Beauty Submits To Her Beast

by

Sydney St. Claire

Once Upon A Dom
Book Four

Beauty Submits To Her Beast

Contact Information: info@thewildrosepress.com

Cover Art by *Diana Carlile*

The Wild Rose Press, Inc.
PO Box 708
Adams Basin, NY 14410-0708

Visit us at www.thewilderroses.com

Publishing History
First Scarlet Rose Edition, 2015
Digital ISBN 978-1-5092-0310-9
Print ISBN 978-1-5092-0995-8

Published in the United States of America

Dedication

With thanks to my editor, Diana Carlile, for her wisdom, insight, dedication and hard work...and gorgeous covers. As my cover artist, I add a huge grateful thanks for the gorgeous covers.

Chapter One

Damon Steele arrived at Pleasure Manor in a mood as foul as the mansion was grand. Another night haunted by the echoing volley of gunfire, screams of men in pain along with images of torn bodies left him edgy and unfit for polite company.

He gripped the steering wheel hard enough to turn his knuckles white. He should just keep going, follow the circular drive past the house, head right back down the long, tree-lined driveway, and return home to his depressing studio apartment where he could wallow in misery. Because he wanted to run, hide, and be alone, he forced himself to park. Bryce Langston, a fellow SEAL and Dom, seldom asked for help, so Damon had driven almost three hours to his friend's country estate.

He stepped out of his truck. The muscle in his left thigh twisted into a tight knot. "Shit." He wheezed out a breath and would have landed on his ass had he not grabbed on to the open door and clung like a man holding on to a floatation device.

Breathing deep, he leaned back, half sitting and half standing. "Should've taken the billionaire up on his offer to send the limo." His injury didn't do so well with long bouts in a car, but he'd figured the drive might hold at bay the nightmare that claimed most of his waking moments and all his nights.

He sucked in air as he stretched his left leg and massaged his thigh, breathing through the painful spasm. The breeze drifted through the trees and swiped across his sweaty brow, the cool hand of a concerned mother checking her child for fever.

His lips twisted. He didn't remember his mother's touch, her voice, or even what she looked like. At age three, he'd been left to the mercy of the state. He'd had many mothers after that, some good, most who took him in for the money. He'd had a nice family once until a new baby arrived and he'd found himself once again on that never-ending circuit of one foster home after another.

Abandoned.

The memories of the boy segued into the nightmare that stalked him day and night—his men trapped, dying, and him unable to save them and get them out.

Abandoned.

He'd been forced to leave them, his brothers in his military family, same as every mother, real or foster, had tossed him aside. The sharp pain in his thigh eased, and before the past could yank him back into the black pit his life had become, he clamped down on his emotions and feelings and stood, refusing to wallow or fall.

Limping more than normal due to muscle spasms and exhaustion, he climbed the steps. A plaque to one side of the dark, double doors proclaimed the residence to be Pleasure Manor. He lifted the large doorknocker. It fell with a resounding crash against the steel plate.

The door opened. A butler in black bowed.

"Welcome, Master Steele."

"Hastings." Damon stepped into a grand foyer and took in the sparkling chandelier, antique furniture, slick marble floor, and a floral arrangement a good four feet tall that graced a gleaming cherrywood table. Wishing he'd brought his cane, he followed the butler. Pride refused to let him use that crutch. He entered a book-lined library where a fire popped and crackled. The warmth of the room wrapped around him with the comfort of an old, worn quilt while the quiet elegance soothed his jangled nerves.

"Master Steele," Hastings announced him.

Bryce rose from a long, dark table dotted with files, maps, and paper. He strode forward, hand outstretched. The two men shook. "Good to see you, Damon. I appreciate you coming here. Glorie and I have a meeting here in less than an hour, one we hope you'll stay and join."

"Always a pleasure to visit your little cottage in the country." His tone was facetious as the place was a huge mansion complete with turrets and impressive grounds, which included woods and real cottages.

He bowed to the dark-haired woman seated at the table. "Mistress." He gave Glorie Amadori the title she deserved. Her formidable reputation as a Domme and powerful businesswoman intimidated most men, even other Doms.

She inclined her head. "How are you, Damon?"

"Surviving." That one word summed up the last few years of his life. He glanced away. The woman had the uncanny ability to see deep into a person's soul, and he was far too vulnerable at the moment. He lowered himself into a leather chair, grateful to be off his aching leg.

Hastings set a thick mug of coffee in front of him, then left the room.

"What's up?" He eyed the pair of Doms.

"Need a favor." Bryce shifted papers and folders.

Damon stretched out his legs. He had a good idea what his old pal needed or wanted. "You want me to take part in one of your events."

"Yes. I need another Dom for a three-day event coming up."

He lifted the mug of coffee. "Don't tell me there isn't anyone willing?" An invitation to Bryce's mansion was an honor. Damon couldn't see very many Doms refusing a weekend of role-play.

Bryce chuckled. "Got a waiting list a mile long, but this sub is new. I need someone I can trust with this one."

Surprised, Damon regarded his friends. "You're allowing newbies?"

"There are several this time, including my sub."

Damon nudged his half-empty coffee aside and lifted a brow. "You're participating?" His friend hadn't taken part in his own events since losing his beloved wife to cancer.

"Yeah." Though Bryce's voice was matter-of-fact, there was a grim set to his mouth and his teal-colored eyes hardened.

Damon sensed there was more to it than just taking on a new sub, but he didn't ask. "Much as I'd like to help you out, I can't." He had a rule—no overnighters. Since his injury, he hadn't slept with a woman. Enjoy a night of sex, yes, but sleep, no.

Bryce picked up a file and tapped it on the corner of the table. "When are you going to forgive yourself? What happened to your men wasn't your fault."

Damon jumped to his feet, then hissed as pain shot through his thigh. "Fuck that. I was their commanding officer, and I left them behind."

Standing, Bryce glared at him. "Hell with that. You were under heavy fire. That shell took out your entire team. Had they not pulled you out, you'd have died."

Thinking of the widows and their children brought guilt and grief to the forefront. "It should have been me," he ground out. "Mike, Eric, Robert, and Manny had families. Should have ordered them to go. To save themselves. They came back for me. They came back and died." He'd never forget the blast that shook the ground, the shrapnel, and the screaming.

"Bullshit. The blame lies with the enemy, not you. It's a risk every SEAL, hell, every soldier takes when we swear an oath to our country."

"Yeah, but you got yourself and your men out." He and Bryce met in the service, trained as SEALs and went on several missions together before each commanded their own group of well-trained men sent into hot spots wherever and whenever needed. Bryce had walked away at the end of his time while Damon reenlisted. He'd served twelve selfless years just to be given the boot. A fist slammed on the table.

"Fuck it, Damon. You didn't fail. Someday you'll realize that and quit kicking yourself in the ass."

"Enough." Glorie's quiet but authoritative voice broke through the air of thick emotion. "Time is ticking. The others will be here soon."

Bryce snagged a folder from his desk and removed a photograph, which he handed to Damon. "This is Caitlin Olsen." He tossed the file onto the table. It slid across, stopped falling over the edge by the mug.

Damon stared at a close-up of a brown-haired woman sitting on horseback. His breath caught in his throat. She glanced over her shoulder at him as though he'd just called her name. Humor brightened her lively, golden eyes, and her mouth curved in a wide smile. For an instant, there was just the two of them sharing a warm, happy, private moment.

She sat in the saddle, her posture straight and commanding, head high, telling him she was a woman in charge and in control and used to issuing orders and having them obeyed. She held the reins in one gloved hand while the other was frozen in mid-stroke on the horse's neck.

Gentle strength. What would it feel like to have those hands touching him, her eyes on him as though he were the only person in her world? He shook off the crazy notion, yet he couldn't glance away.

Her humor and love of life mesmerized him, but beneath it all, her gaze was deep and penetrating. This woman didn't miss much. His fingers tightened on the photo, and he resisted the urge to trace her features with his finger. He needed to see her, longed to hear her laughter and surround himself with her earthy beauty and vitality.

Damon stumbled back and dropped into his chair. "I don't work with new subs. You know that." God, but he wanted this one.

Bryce resumed his seat. "Caitlin's had a tough time of it. Raised two younger siblings while caring for her mother who had MS. Glorie and I have each interviewed her. She owns a horse ranch. She's strong-willed, used to being in charge."

Damon set the photo onto the table, yet he couldn't tear his eyes from hers. "Sounds like she's more Domme than sub."

"Or a woman who yearns to give up control in one area of her life," Glorie put in. "The theme for the three day event is Fairytales." She grinned and added, "*Fairytales your mother never read you.* If you agree to partner Caitlin, she'll be Belle."

He lifted a brow. "Who is Belle?"

Bryce laughed. "Need to freshen up on your bedtime stories, bro. Belle from *Beauty and the Beast.*"

For a long moment, Damon held his friend's gaze, aware of the ironic mirroring of his life to that fairytale. His glanced back at the photo. *Shit.* She was definitely a beauty, and he himself was pretty beastly these days, a wounded war hero according to government. Curious despite himself, he grabbed his cooling coffee and snagged the folder. He took a sip and opened the file. And choked as he swallowed.

A picture of Caitlin, wearing a skimpy bustier,

greeted him. "Fuck!" His breath caught in his throat as he stared at a much different image of her. She was leaning against a tall bedpost, hands over her head, wrists tied with a scarf. Her tits were bare, the nipples a deep, rosy red and puckered, begging for a man to suck and lick. But what had his heart pounding and his dick stirring was the way she rested one foot on the bed, revealing her dark mound with just a hint of pink showing.

"Damn." His gaze shifted from her body to her face. The pose was supposed to be inviting, sexy and enticing, yet the uncertainty lurking in those large, expressive cat-like eyes spoke to a part of him he thought long dead.

Damon glanced from Bryce to Glorie, then stared at Caitlin Olsen. It'd be a cold day in hell before he allowed another Dom to introduce her to the BDSM lifestyle.

****

Three weeks later

"Caitlin Olsen, what the hell are you doing?" Caitie stared at herself in the mirror. She wore a low cut blue dress with a white apron and matching blue and white feathered mask. The woman staring back at her was a stranger. She was dressed as though she were on her way to a Halloween party, except she'd never wear anything so revealing in public.

The fabric of the dress was practically sheer. Thank god for the apron in the front, but there was no hiding her dark, pouty tips. If that wasn't bad enough, the bodice was so low, if she sneezed, her girls would bounce right out. She tugged at the elastic neckline, tried to tuck herself in more securely, but the design was meant to reveal, not cover.

She bit her lower lip and whirled around in front of the mirror to eye the back of her dress. The points of the handkerchief hem swirled just below her ass. In the bright light, she could see the outline of her butt. Per instructions, she wore no bra. She flushed. And no panties. "Shit. Hope you don't have to bend over, Caitie-girl."

From a pocket in her apron, she drew a thick, creamy-yellow invitation. A banner style logo stretched across the top. In the center, an embossed, metallic blue castle gleamed with the words *The Kingdom of Dom* in a fancy, swirly script. She scanned the invite.

You are hereby invited to Pleasure Manor for a weekend of pure pleasure.

Pure pleasure. She shivered with anticipation. She was thirty, yet she was as excited as a horny teen. Sex hadn't been part of her life for far too many years. She'd been too busy raising her much younger siblings and caring for her invalid mother. Now she was on her own.

She didn't have time to date, and online dating services weren't for her. Too risky. Besides, her ranch, For the Love of Horses, took most of her time and energy. She had her pick of men. One couldn't own a ranch without lots of hunky, brawny men to help work it, but she had a rule. No sex with the hired hands, no matter how good-looking. Too many complications. She'd learned that miserable lesson the hard way. So she'd allowed her friend to talk her into trying a weekend BDSM role-play.

With a complete stranger.

She let out a groan.

A stranger. What had she been thinking?

No strings. No emotional involvements. No jealousy and no tantrums.

Her last boyfriend had worked for her and had been jealous of the men on the ranch, yet any time they went to a bar, he'd flirt outrageously with the waitresses and barmaids. She'd lost too many hired hands due to fights and threats before she'd broken up with Larry and kicked his two-timing ass off her ranch.

And now, here she was in a mansion called Pleasure Manor where orgasms were handed out like candy on Halloween, according to her good friend. It wasn't Halloween, but the event had sounded like fun, so here she was, eager to gather a bagful of goodies. Except she was hiding in the ladies' lounge with her second thoughts.

She studied her costume. For the next three days, if she didn't chicken out, she was Belle. But who was the Beast she'd agreed to submit to in return for sex?

She laughed. No one who knew her would ever call her a submissive woman. She wasn't some wimp eager to play doormat to any man, nor was she the type to jump into bed with a stranger. Lord knew, she hated bar hopping with her friend Maize. She shuddered. Too many slimy creeps out there. So what was she doing here?

Both Bryce and Glorie, the host and hostess of the event had suggested that she had a deep, inner need to be submissive, to give up control in one area of her life. She rolled her eyes as she finger-combed her hair. She didn't think so, yet she'd agreed to submit to this man as though she were his sex slave.

"Sex. Slave." A hum of desire swam through her bloodstream like an alligator sliding into the river to hunt prey. Since signing up for the event, she'd had lots of fantasies of her dream hunk driving her wild and giving her one orgasm after another. An arrow of lust set off the throbbing deep in her center. Damn, she was wet just thinking about it.

The door to the lounge opened. A woman in a black uniform with a white apron poked her head inside. "Hey, you'd better get in there with the others."

Caitie whirled around, relieved to see her friend. "Good God, Maize," she said. "I must have been crazy to let you talk me into this? I don't know anything about this BDSM stuff. Or being submissive."

Not beyond what she'd researched on-line. She pressed her fist into her stomach to still the sick, panicking feeling welling up inside. "I've never even read *Fifty Shades of Grey*." But listening to her friend go on and on about how wonderful it was to hand over control to a man and get pleasured in returned made her long to experience what Maize referred to as the incredible and never-ending weekend of orgasms.

Maize flounced into the room, her short, black skirt bouncing. "You'll love it, Caitie. Give your Dom a chance. Just think about the wild and kinky sex and lots and lots of delicious orgasms."

Pacing, Caitie chewed her lower lip. "It's the kinky sex I'm worried about." She whirled around. "I don't know this guy, not even his name."

The maid grinned. "Identities are protected. That's why everyone wears masks."

"You're not wearing a mask."

She giggled. "That's 'cause I'm part of the staff."

Caitie narrowed her eyes, stepped back, and crossed her arms, then groaned when one breast popped out of her top. She adjusted the neckline. "Why aren't you participating if this is so much fun?"

Maize preened in front of the mirror. "Who said I'm not?" She wagged her brows. "Have you any idea what pleasures that butler can give an innocent maid in the pantry, girlfriend?"

She held up her hand. "Don't tell me. Don't need to know."

"Come on. You best join the others."

With one last glance in the mirror, Caitie followed Maize to a formal parlor.

"Have fun, Belle." Her friend closed the door behind her.

Chapter Two

Caitie clasped her hands in front of her, pressing her fists into her stomach to still the nervous fluttering. She had a choice. Stick with the plan or run like hell. She took stock of her surroundings. She'd never seen such a richly appointed room. Everything sparkled or glittered. Antiques, gilt frames, and even a baby grand in the corner all spoke of wealth. Tall windows along one wall let in light and kept the room from being dark and oppressive. A pair of French doors stood open to allow the warm, afternoon breeze to enter.

It took her a moment to realize guys were on one side of the room and the women on the other. No mingling. Her gaze swept over the men, and damn, if her temperature didn't spike at the sight of so many hunky bodies on display. Some of them were covered from neck to shoes in rich, velveteen tunics and pants and appeared quite princely and commanding while others were attired in very little. She stared at a man wearing in a wolfish mask. Her eyes lowered. He wore a form-fitting leather glove over his huge dick. She barely swallowed her gasp of shock but couldn't stop her face from burning with embarrassment.

OMG. That was one prime hunk. Was he her beast? She could get on board having him for the next few days, but then she noticed his attention was wholly focused on a woman in a red dress and cape. Okay, Red and her Wolf. She got that.

She continued her perusal of the weekend's offerings. At the end of the line, three men huddled together. Like a moth drawn to a dangerous flame, she eyed the first who stood with his back to her. Her gaze slid down to his naked, white-as-snow ass. *Oh, ick.* His ass sagged, reminding her of an overinflated balloon that had lost its air. She resisted the urge to slap her hands over her eyes. Barely.

The second had a nice butt. He turned toward her. He wore a furry mask, a studded collar, and leather straps that formed a harness over his pale chest. He was rail thin, had the start of a potbelly, and oh, sweet Jesus, just a bit of cloth to hide his crotch. He grinned at her. She nearly screamed and ran from the room like a frightened schoolgirl. The third wasn't bad. He had a nice bum, at least, but was way too hairy for her.

God, not him. Please not him or the other two with him. If I have to have sex with a stranger, please let him be a man in good, physical shape.

"You're new, aren't you?"

So engrossed, or rather, so grossed out, Caitie hadn't heard the woman approach. She smiled. "How can you tell?" Her voice sounded high and choked.

Her companion laughed, grabbed her arm, and then led her to the other end of the room. "I'm Rapunzel. Come join us." She leaned close. "We're feasting on the men from down here. Well, some of them."

Appreciating the humor, Caitie eyed the woman's long, blonde hair. It fell like a sheet of molten gold past her butt. She smiled. "They going to lock you in one of those turrets?"

"I sure hope so." She indicated a woman in a silky, sexy white nightgown. "This is Wendy."

"Ah, your partner is Peter Pan."

"Nope. Captain Hook." She tossed her dark, blonde head and jerked her chin toward a man wearing an elaborate eye patch that masked half his face.

Caitie let out a low sound of appreciation. "He does look like a strong seafaring captain." The man's shoulders were broad, his waist narrow. He wore a leather vest that hung open and leather pants and boots. He had a magnificent chest. Aware of the women staring at him, he shoved his hands onto his hips and planted his feet apart.

"Don't see his hook," she whispered.

Wendy giggled. "Not looking in the right spot. Lower, sweetie. All he has to do is whip that bad boy out, and he's hooked me."

The women laughed. Rapunzel nudged the other woman in their group. "This is Goldilocks. Goldie here is going to have fun with her three bears."

"Three? At once?" Caitie blushed when everyone laughed at her shocked expression.

"Hell, yes." The mask didn't hide the gleam in her eyes.

"Definitely a newbie," a dry voice inserted.

Caitie glanced at the newcomer and met the

amused gaze of a woman wearing a black mask and skimpy, black bustier. The woman swished her riding crop against her black stockings and lifted a brow.

"Evil Fairy from *Sleeping Beauty*," the woman in black introduced herself.

Rapunzel grinned and leaned close. "She's a Domme. She's going to be doing the spanking this weekend."

"Spanking?" Caitie's voice rose to a squeak. No one said anything about spankings. She eyed the crop. *Or whips.*

"And a whole lot of riding." The evil fairy smiled fiercely.

The women around Caitie chuckled. She gave a weak smile. Maize had some explaining to do. In the meantime, she'd make it clear to her partner that there would be no pain. None. Zip. Zero.

The Domme ran the tip of her riding crop across the tops of Caitie's breasts. "And you are…Sleeping Beauty?"

"No. Belle."

"Ah." The evil fairy scanned the men. "Don't see your beast."

"There is that wickedly delicious wolf there." Rapunzel licked her lips.

"I believe he has his little playmate already." The evil fairy indicated the woman in the red satin cloak.

Once again, Caitie tried to guess which of the deliciously sexy men was hers as she listened to the banter of the women. As more people joined the participants, Caitie and the others made a game of guessing what role each would play and which hunk belonged to which woman.

She'd pegged Red Riding Hood and Cinderella. And blushed when Mary and Little Bo Peep entered. If she thought her costume revealing, Bo's skirt was nonexistent in the back and she wore only a red thong. And what a relief that the two women boldly claimed the three men huddled together like a flock of sheep. Caitie thanked the gods that they were taken out of the running.

She scanned the room again and noted that people were getting restless. Anticipation and lust filled the air. "What are we waiting for?"

"For the queen, of course," Rapunzel said.

At that moment, the doors opened and the butler stepped inside to announce, "Queen Grimhilde."

A tall woman entered. Her black corset pushed her breasts up and out, and a sheer, lacy skirt with red accents barely covered her crotch in front. Four men in skintight leather followed. Each wore a full mask. Silence fell. Caitie recognized Glorie Amadori. Everything about her screamed Domme, and she admitted to finding Glorie a very scary Domme at that.

"Good afternoon, my lovely subjects. I'm Queen Grimhilde, Snow White's evil stepmother, and as I survey all of you gathered in this room, I declare that I am still the fairest in all the land."

Caitie laughed, and her nerves settled as the hostess gave out instructions. Everyone seemed friendly, at ease, and eager to begin. She slid her gaze along the line of women. Well, except for

Cinderella. She seemed nervous, and Caitie had the feeling she was as new to this as she was.

"You will each be shown to your quarters for the weekend. Please respect your boundaries. Other couples are also sharing the mansion and grounds. My guards will be on the prowl if anyone has any problems or questions. If you leave the privacy of your rooms or cottages, make sure you wear your masks. We'll meet as a group in the ballroom Saturday evening for the ball. Until then, remember: Safe, sane, and consensual."

The Queen called couples and sent them on their way. The wolf claimed Red, Cinderella was taken away by one of the guards, as was Snow White, after the queen taunted her *dearest stepdaughter*. Captain Hook swept Wendy off her feet. Caitie laughed with the others and relaxed. *Okay, this was going to be fun.*

When her name was called, Rapunzel stepped forward. A prince stepped forward as well and was ordered to take his sub to the tower and keep her there until she learned her place. He did so by throwing Rapunzel over his shoulder.

Caitie's jaw dropped when the Dom ran his hands over the woman's bared ass. Her face burned with embarrassment. Some guy did that to her in public, he wouldn't be walking for a week.

"Belle."

Caitie squared her shoulders and stepped forward, tilting her chin, calling upon a control that had even the toughest horse wrangler on her ranch ready to run if she even mouthed the word.

"Kneel before your queen."

Keeping her features schooled, Caitie knelt, as Red had knelt before the wolf.

"Head down and hands behind your back, sub."

This was part of the game, part of the role she was to play, so she did as commanded and submitted to the queen.

"Very good. You understand that for the next three days you are under the obligation to do whatever your Dom orders?"

"Yes."

"Yes, Mistress."

Caitlin drew in a deep breath. How bad did she want a weekend of wild sex and a smorgasbord of orgasms? Enough to answer meekly, "Yes, Mistress."

"You were given instructions on using safewords. Do you understand what a safeword is and how to use it?"

"The safeword is red. It is used to stop all play."

"Correct. Play stops to allow you and your Dom to discuss your fears or concerns. The guards are monitors, and it's their task to assist if there are problems. You'll be escorted to your cell where your Beast awaits. Are you ready for the games to begin?"

Caitie let out her breath. "Yes, Mistress." Good heavens. For good or bad, she was here and she was going to do this.

"You may stand, but keep your head down and hands behind you."

It was awkward to get to her feet without revealing herself to the two men standing at attention in front of her.

The queen circled Caitlin, then slid her hands down her arms. Something soft snapped around each wrist.

Caitie's head shot up. "Hey!" She yanked at her wrists, shocked to find herself cuffed like a common criminal. She glared at the queen. "Take them off."

Glorie lifted one brow. "Your Dom wishes you to be bound. This is your first lesson in giving up your need to control."

Panic ran through Caitie. Her heart raced. "I agreed to give up control for sex. I didn't agree to this." She'd read that bondage was part of the BDSM lifestyle, but she'd also figured she had the right to choose whether or not to be bound.

Chuckling, Glorie beckoned one of her guards to join them. "My sweet, handsome slave, what happens to subs when they are disobedient and defiant?"

"My queen, a sub who does not obey is punished." His eyes gleamed with desire.

"Shall we demonstrate?" She ran her crop over his bare chest and trailed the tip lower, across his crotch.

"Yes, Mistress." The man spun around, bent over, hands clasped around his ankles as he presented his ass to the queen.

Caitie gulped. Shit, he had a smooth, tanned ass and lots of dark, curly hair from his thighs, to, well, everywhere. Glorie drew a short riding crop from her belt. With a quick flick of her wrist, the whip swished through the air and struck one finely muscled cheek. A thin, red line appeared. The spit in Caitie's mouth dried, and she widened her eyes. When the man straightened, and shifted to face them, the silky sack cupping his penis was stretched taut.

The queen ran the tip of the whip along his erection. "You, my lovely sub, liked that entirely too much." The queen's voice was a low tease.

The huntsman bowed his head. "Yes, Mistress. I confess. I like it when you punish me."

Chuckling, the queen returned to Caitie. She trailed the tip of the whip across her shoulder and traced circles around each hidden nipple. "That is what happens to subs who do not show proper respect or who do not obey their Doms, so have a care. You are not my sub, therefore, you are not mine to discipline." She feathered a finger along Caitie's jawline. "Too bad." Caitie was relieved until the queen added, "In that manner. But punished you must be."

Before she could protest, the woman yanked her top down and tucked the elastic neckline beneath one full breast. "Say nothing. This is your first lesson in learning to accept dominance. Accepting my discipline shows your compliance. And respect."

Embarrassed to have two men staring at her bare boob, Caitie lowered her gaze and swallowed hard. "I can use the safeword, right?"

The tip of the whip tapped beneath her chin. She lifted her head and met the queens amused gaze. "No. As I said, this is your first lesson. Your only choice is to accept or decide this weekend event isn't for you and leave. From this point on, you are bound by the rules, rules you agreed to in writing. If you have changed your mind, speak now. Do you wish to stay and participate?"

Caitie's eyes shifted to the door at the back of the room. A third Huntsman entered and joined the other two. Great, now three men were eying her bared breast. She drew in a deep breath and made her decision. She was here. She wasn't going to chicken out. "Yes, Mistress."

The queen nodded. "Take her to the dungeon where her Beast awaits."

Caitie didn't dare speak, but she couldn't help feeling angry and humiliated as she was led down a flight of stairs and along a long, darkened corridor toward a set of double doors.

Chapter Three

What was he thinking? Damon paced in front of the fireplace and winced when his thigh tightened painfully. Stopping, he stared at the flickering pillar candles that replaced burning wood. He never took on new subs, preferring women who knew the score, but one glance at his weekend sub, and he had to have her.

For years, he'd existed, survived by going through the motions of living. He often likened himself as one of the walking dead. Everything he'd been before that last mission had been either destroyed or left behind with his team of men who'd lost their lives.

But something about Caitlin Olsen's photo had sparked a tiny flame in the dark cavity of his heart, mind, and soul. Why? She was beautiful, no getting around that. He'd have to be truly dead not to appreciate her classic beauty—her large, expressive eyes, full lips, and curvy body—but he also acknowledged there was more to her than looks.

Thinking of his role for the weekend, he grimaced. In the fairytale, the Beast was an ugly, deformed man spurned by society, and Damon…he was an injured war hero hiding his beast deep inside with his dark moods.

In the movie, Belle tamed her beast with

unconditional love and acceptance, and the beast overcame his curse and became a prince once again. Damon had no such expectations. He'd never been and never would be a prince.

The door to the spacious suite of rooms opened. He shifted from staring into the candle flames. His heart thumped hard as he got his first look at Caitlin Olsen in person. And what a first glance.

She held her head high as she stormed into the sitting room. Her eyes beneath her mask glittered with anger and resentment, those full, sexy lips were compressed into a flat, tight line, and she had one glorious tit exposed. Her skirt swished around her thighs, and her sheer top teased him with the dark shadow of her other breast. More than her body, it was her face that struck him speechless.

Sweet Jesus walking on water! The woman was wild, earthy, and totally unlike any sub he'd taken on. Every stiff line screamed a silent challenge, including the tipping of her chin and the glare in her sparking, golden eyes.

He deliberately lowered his gaze to her exposed tit. He sucked in his gut and swallowed hard. Talk about beauty and perfection. It took every ounce of control not to go to her and cup that perfect mound in his palm and flick his fingers across her dark, dusky nipple. His dick stirred, and suddenly, he was eager to begin his role of Dom.

Aware of her displeasure at his open admiration, he hid his grin, seeing Glorie's hand in his sub's exposed state. His gaze returned to her face. From the anger in her features, he'd guess she'd challenged the Queen of Dommes. And lost.

So why was this obviously strong willed woman willing to take on a submissive role? Bryce and Glorie just might be wrong in their assessment of Caitlin. The challenge in her eyes ignited an answering need in him to peel away those layers and find that hidden sub—if she existed.

He straightened, planted his feet apart, and clasped his hands behind his back. The weekend ahead should prove enlightening and entertaining. And a distraction from his own dark moods and thoughts. He suspected that taming this sub would take all his wits.

****

Hot damn. Instead of a beast, Lady Fate gifted her with her very own god.

The man leaning against the mantle was one hell of a hunk from the top of his dark, auburn head to his bare feet. Unlike the men in the parlor, he didn't wear a mask. He was good looking, but not in a pretty-boy or young exec manner. His face was too tough and hard. The lines etched around his eyes and mouth spoke of someone who'd seen and experienced more of life than most.

Judging from his firm jaw—holy cow, her heart gave a couple hard thumps at the sight of a deep chin dent and lord knew, she had a weakness for a man with a cleft chin—he was not a doormat. Her heart raced. The buzz of attraction swirled in her head, then swept through her body like a whirlwind. She curled her toes, ran her tongue over her front teeth, and let herself absorb her prize for three, delicious days.

Her gaze traced across his mile-wide shoulders,

then traveled over his bronzed, muscular chest. His leather vest hung open, and her fingers itched to comb through his thick mat of dark curly hair with a reddish glint to find his twin nipples. With his bod, they were sure to be yummy and sexy as hell.

Her first fear of being stuck with a playmate well past his prime flew out the window. This man playing Beast to her Belle stood straight and tall as though he were in the military and could have stepped off a dude ranch or, considering his attire, the glossy spread of a sex magazine. No wimpy, pale, thin guy with a saggy ass and potbelly for her. Her fingers tingled with the urge to touch and explore. And claim.

He remained silent and still as her gaze traveled from his flat abdomen to the soft and buttery leather chaps snugged low on his hips and buckled around each tree-trunk thigh. Yum. Definitely cowboy material. Too bad she didn't have someone like him on her ranch. Her rule of no dating the ranch hands would go right out the window. Or barn if she got him into the loft.

And OMG—her heart once again thumped hard against her ribs—his costume had no crotch. As she'd seen in the parlor upstairs, he too wore a G-string sack to hide his goodies and judging from the strain on the fabric, he had prime, yummy man parts.

That first delicious shiver of pure lust morphed to raging need that flooded between her legs like a fall of water crashing into a pool. *Wow*. Her anger at being cuffed against her will, along with the embarrassment at having a boob hanging out faded as she met his intense steel-blue eyes. She stared at his full, sexy mouth and hoped he was a good kisser. His mouth begged to be kissed.

She licked her lips, suddenly nervous again. How did a person begin a cold turkey sexual fling? She didn't engage in one-night stands, always dated and got to know her past lovers first. "I'm Caitlin. I've never been here before. What now?" She knew what she wanted to do—make use of that sofa.

He inclined his head. "I'm Damon. I'll be your Dom for the weekend. Find the X on the floor and stand on it."

Damon. To tame. Oh, yes, she wanted to tame her beast. Like a flame set to gas-soaked briquettes, his gaze on her breast, along with his sexy, deep baritone voice, ignited the ball of lust swirling in her center.

Whew, this won't be so bad. In fact, if she hadn't been cuffed, she might have jumped him, tumbled them both onto the couch.

He snapped his fingers, bringing her back to the here and now. "First rule. I don't give instructions more than once. Do as I ordered."

Caitie sucked in her breath. The lust in her veins cooled and once again, indignation threaded with anger took hold. "Excuse me?" No one had ordered her around since she was thirteen and assumed the role of parent to her younger siblings and caregiver to her mother.

"Your choice is to obey or leave. If you want to leave, I'll remove the cuffs and let Hastings arrange for you to be taken home."

Go before she sampled this hunk? Nope.

Wouldn't happen, no matter how much she hated being told what to do. So far, the weekend wasn't what she'd imagined, but her curiosity was piqued, and her body ached to have this man kiss her. And fuck her like a stallion claiming his mare. This Belle wanted her Beast.

She gave her surroundings a quick glance. The cozy sitting room held a sofa and chair. Overhead lights ran on tracks across the ceiling. Several silk plants overhead added color to the corners, and the candles in the fireplace added warmth and comfort. She spotted an X taped to the floor. A pot of ivy hung from the track lighting. Too bad, mistletoe would have been very fitting.

Head high, shoulders back, she did as ordered and planted her feet on the X. "Fine. Now what?"

Damon left the mantel, willed himself not to limp as he called upon his military training to ignore and overcome the dull throbbing in his thigh. Nothing was going to interfere with his weekend. He removed her mask, and his gaze held hers. "Very good. I expect obedience from my subs." He trailed one finger across the creamy swell of her breast and circled her puckered nipple until it shrank and tightened into a jutting peak. "Why are you walking around with your tit exposed?" He closed his palm over her breast and squeezed.

A streak of heat burned beneath his touch. It was strange, wrong even, to allow a perfect stranger to fondle her so intimately without a chance of getting to know him, but obviously, they were here for sex and he planned to get right to it. And that was fine with her. Caitie thrust her chest forward, pushing her breast fully into his hand. "Wasn't my idea. That woman cuffed me, and then pulled my top down."

Her weekend hunk tweaked her nipple hard.

"Hey!" She sucked in a breath, stemming her cry of pleasure as lust exploded deep in her core like a dormant volcano flaring to life.

"That woman is your queen and your hostess. You will show her proper respect. Understand?"

Caitie didn't dare roll her eyes. She bit back her sigh and glanced away as she nodded.

He tapped her chin with his finger. "The correct response is, yes, Sir."

Her gaze returned to his. "Excuse me?" She'd forgotten that Doms were accorded such lordly titles. She grimaced. It'd been one thing to address the queen as Mistress, but she'd never yes sirred a man in her life. The words stuck in her throat.

"I am your Dom, and you are my sub. You will answer yes, Sir, or yes, Master."

Or leave.

He didn't say it, but it was in his eyes and in the firm set to those full, sexy lips. She'd read about Doms and subs on-line, but it hadn't occurred to her that it was going to be real. She'd assumed the event was just an excuse for a bunch of people to gather and play make believe in order to engage in wild sex. Besides, she wasn't a real sub. One glance at the man so casually fondling her breast said he considered himself the real deal.

So how badly did she want to make love with Damon? Enough to overcome her aversion to being a good, meek, obedient little girl? She chewed the inside of her cheeks. Yeah. Master was out, though. That left her with the equally distasteful, Sir.

"Fine. *Yes, Sir*. I understand."

Damon chuckled. "You don't, but by the end of the weekend, you will. Now, back to the question. Explain this." He pinched her exposed nipple.

Caitie bit her lower lip to stop her whimper as the tingling in her breast echoed deep beneath her clit. She was already so damn wet and wanted to get to the wild sex and orgasm smorgasbord part of the menu. "I protested when she cuffed me without asking, then told her to take them off."

Damon laughed, his eyes crinkling as the first hint of humor warmed those steely blues. "Now that, little sub, is something I'd have liked to have seen. Be grateful she didn't spank you on the spot."

Caitie wrinkled her nose. "She whipped one of her guards, showing me what happens to subs who don't obey." Caitie worried her lower lip. "I'm not into that stuff. Or any pain."

Damon lifted a brow.

"Sir."

He nodded. "You have much to learn. It's my duty for the next three days to instruct you about the BDSM world and your role as a sub. If you accept, you'll discover things about yourself you never knew." He trailed his finger across the top of her breast to the other.

She shivered with anticipation, eager to experience this man's touch. He cupped both breasts, and she wished he'd bare them both.

"I will push you past your comfort zone, make demands, and expect obedience. In return, you'll be pleasured beyond anything you've experienced."

Oh, my god.

Pleasured beyond anything you've experienced. The promise spun her insides to goo. She swayed toward him.

Damon removed his hands and strode behind her. He shifted so close, the heat from his body seeped into hers. "Let's get some basic housekeeping out of the way, my sweet Belle. The envelopes containing our blood results are on the table. Everyone must have a clean bill of health."

"That's good to know," she said, her voice low and throaty.

"According to your questionnaire, you've never experienced any BDSM role-play. Did you read the guide you were given, and do you understand the role and use of safewords?"

"Yes, Sir. I did a lot of research on the internet, and the queen also made sure I understood. If I don't like something, I say the word *red*, and you'll stop."

"Correct. I'll halt all play, and we'll discuss what you didn't like and why. In your research, did you come across anything you consider a definite no?"

She chewed on her lower lip. "Pain is out. Not into the sado stuff, so no whips or canes." She wrinkled her nose. "Some of the pictures of women tied up with ropes were scary looking as well."

"Fair enough. Let's set some boundaries. Because you're new, I'd hate for you to discount many of pleasurable activities without having the experience necessary to make an informed decision.

For now, we'll say the use of gentle bondage is acceptable—cuffs or a silk scarf—and we'll give light spanking a try."

Her jaw dropped. "Spanking?" She whipped her head to the side to glare at him.

"Face forward." He waited until she complied. "We'll stick with the flat of the hand. Or a paddle."

Caitie's breath caught in her throat. "I—"

"Why are you participating in this event?" He stroked his hands across her shoulders and down her arms.

She struggled to get her mind around the possibility of being spanked. She licked her lips. "My friend Maize said the sex is great and orgasms are handed out like candy at Halloween." She moaned when his palms slid over her wrists. His fingers trailed across the center of her palms, making her shiver. Her fingers curled over his. Then he cupped her ass with his warm hands. "I—um— love sweets." Her voice slithered into a moan, and she wiggled her hips, seeking more, wanting more.

He chuckled. "As do I. We'll just pretend that tonight is Halloween. I've got a lot of fun activities planned for our party." His breath swirled in her ear. "You've agreed to take part in what we call a Total Power Exchange. Tell me what that means?" The tip of his tongue traced a vein in her neck, and he shifted even closer, his hard thighs pressing against her buttocks, his hands sliding around to grip her hips.

The tips of her fingers brushed against his bare abdomen. She felt the tickle of his pubic hair and sucked in a breath. Did he want her as much as she wanted him? The insides of her thighs grew uncomfortably damp as her body hummed with need. She ached deep in her center and, between her legs, her clit throbbed. Damn, she longed for him to bend her over and slide his cock into her pussy. Forget warm ups and foreplay. She'd take it hard and fast.

A squeeze of his hands reminded her she hadn't answered his question. "It means you're in charge, and I have to do whatever you say." God, the thought of obeying this man turned her on.

"You're partially correct," he said, his voice a low rumble in her ear. "Think of domination in a relationship as perceived control. The trust bond between Doms and subs requires submission from both parties to be truly mutual and balanced.

"I, as a Dom, gain power from a sub's submissiveness. You, as a submissive, gain power by giving up all your worry, all your cares and fears. You are handing me total control over you, and when I accept, I am wholly responsible for you." Damon licked and nibbled his way along her collarbone.

Caitie tipped her head to one side. His hands wrapped around her waist and rested low on her belly. The heat of his body made thinking difficult. If only he'd trail those fingers lower and touch her where she throbbed and pulsed. "Um, how does that make you submissive?"

"Not submissive. Submission, as I will put aside all my wants and needs for you. For the next three days, you'll be my total focus. That means I'll take charge of each of our play sessions. It is now my duty and responsibility to pleasure you and meet all your needs. All I require of you is to let go of all inhibitions and enjoy each new experience."

His warm and spicy scent wrapped around her like cotton protecting a fragile object while his voice, low and compelling, lured her into relaxing against him.

"Will you trust me, Belle, give up all your worries, and hand over any shame or preconceived ideas and beliefs? Will you give yourself permission to experience and feel and believe that I know what your body wants and needs?" His hands stroked up and, once again, closed over her breasts, one bare, the other covered.

Caitie sucked in her breath. Could she give a perfect stranger total control? Pure lust ran like liquid gold through her, and when he tweaked each nipple, then rolled the sensitive bud between his fingers, her knees nearly buckled. She wasn't sure she could surrender to the extent he demanded, but she definitely wanted this man to make love to her.

"I'll try," she moaned, turning to offer him her mouth.

"Wrong answer." Damon stepped away, leaving her achy, cold, and so alone. "If you forget the rules, I stop."

Oh, god, don't stop.

He grasped her shoulders, flipped her around, and fixed intense, steely blues on her. "You either comply or you don't. Either you trust me or you do not. What is your answer?"

Could she put herself in his hands? She stared deep into his eyes. There was something there.

Buried. A reserve. A part of him he kept hidden. More, she sensed he needed, truly needed, not just wanted her to trust him. In that moment, he reminded her of the abused, neglected, and abandoned horses she took in, animals no one wanted or cared about. She recognized a wounded animal when she saw one. And that was all it took for her to draw in a deep breath and answer, "Yes, Sir. I trust you."

"Will you give me everything I ask or demand? All or nothing, little sub. You will surrender totally. Say it."

"God, yes. I surrender. Totally. Sir." Caitlin tipped her head back, lips parted in silent plea. She struggled against the cuffs. "I want to touch you. Take off the cuffs." She added a belated, Sir."

Damon lifted a brow. Caitlin intrigued and enchanted him, and he couldn't say why. He appreciated her spirited nature and understood her need for control. She'd both surrendered and issued an order in the same breath. He hid his amusement. His sub didn't understand what it meant to surrender, and by god, he would enjoy teaching her the meaning of submissive.

The hard knot in his belly loosened, making him realize he'd been afraid she'd refuse him. Still holding her gaze, he noted how desire had changed her eyes from a bright honey brown to the shade of dark, aged whisky.

He eased her top over her covered tit, exposing both breasts. Her sigh pleased him, as did her weight on his palms. She was deliciously heavy, and she more than filled his hands. He lowered his eyes to her full mounds topped with rosy nipples, each drawn tight as though brushed with an icy wind.

Fuck. The jolt of pure lust almost had him falling to his knees. One pale breast mesmerized him. The pair sent a tidal wave of need crashing into his balls with enough force to have him gasping as though he'd just been kicked there. His breath caught in his throat, and his need for this woman nearly wiped out his control. He wanted nothing more than to pick her up like the beast he played and dump her onto the couch so he could suck and nibble until she writhed and begged beneath him. Then he'd fuck her until they were both well sated.

It took effort to still his raging need. Each breath Caitlin drew in caused her chest to swell, and under his palms, her heart pounded. She leaned close, silently begging for more. Though he wanted her, sooner rather than later, his first duty was to her, not to easing his own aches. To remind himself of his promise to her, he rubbed his palms across the turgid tips, loving the way she shivered and bit her lower lip.

"Please, Damon. Sir. I'm ready for you. I ache."

Her confession pleased him, as did the hunger in her expressive eyes. He'd seen defiance there when she entered their suite, laughter in the one photo of her on horseback, and a hint of uncertainty in her sexy, posed picture. Now he needed to see blind need. For him.

"Ready for what, my sweet Belle?" He trapped her pouty tips between thumbs and forefingers then squeezed and pulled. Her surprised gasp became a throaty moan that prowled through him like a panther stalking through a jungle.

She closed her eyes and leaned into him. "That. More. I like your hands on me." She drew in a long, shuddering breath.

"Eyes on me," he commanded as he continued to play with her breasts. She shuddered when he applied gentle pressure to each rosy tip.

"Oh-oh." She gasped and panted and shivered.

"Do you like what I'm doing?" He pinched harder, judging her reaction.

She cried out and squeezed her legs together. "Oh, yes, Sir. More, Sir." Her moan rose to a low cry. "Now enough of all this. Remove these damn cuffs so I can touch you back."

Damon choked, then coughed. Just when he thought he had her where he wanted her, that need of hers to take charge returned. Since entering their suite, she'd challenged him, both verbally and in her demeanor. First task, was to establish some ground rules and teach her what it meant to give him her all.

"Are they hurting you?" Holding her shoulders, he turned her around to examine the fur-lined cuffs. They didn't appear too tight, nor were they chafing her skin. He stroked her hands, her wrists, and her palms, pleased when her fingers curled around his.

She glanced over her shoulder, met his questioning gaze. "No. I just don't like them."

"As they aren't hurting, they stay." Her eyes flashed with annoyance and rebellion, but she kept silent. Oh yeah, she was going to give him a run for his money. For the first time in a long time, excitement hummed through his mind and his body, waking every nerve and cell. The elastic of his cock sack pulled taut as his erection protested confinement.

He pushed her hands up so he could brush his dick against her ass. She gasped and leaned back into him. It nearly killed him to allow her to wiggle against him. Good god, the anticipation was going to be the death of him. Her frustrated exhale when he stepped away mirrored his own response.

"My rules, remember? When and how I say. Let's go over lesson one, which you should have learned upstairs with the queen. Subs do not make demands. You may ask, but as your Dom, I am in charge. From this moment on, until I end this play session, you will do exactly as I say. If you don't, you'll be punished."

"Punished? Like spanked?" Her voice rose an octave.

Damon trailed his hands up her arms, across her shoulders and leaned close enough to feel her breath on his lips. "There are other ways to punish disobedient subs. You are mine for the next three days. I will do what I please with you, when I please, and how I please. Do you understand?" He deepened his voice and scraped his teeth and tongue along the ridge of her shoulder.

She sighed like a contented, purring kitten. "Yes, Sir."

Chuckling, Damon drew her around to face him. His traced the back of his fingers just beneath her jawbone and stared deeply into the liquid gold of her eyes. "You don't, because you don't understand what it means to submit mind and body, but you will, my sweet sub. You will."

He bent his head and claimed her mouth.

Chapter Four

Caitie parted her lips and sighed. *About damn time.* That thought was followed by *holy mother of god.* She'd been right. Her beast had a mouth made for kissing. His lips were warm, soft, and full as they danced and mated with hers.

His hands gripped her shoulders, one arm sliding down to pull her close while the other cradled the back of her head as he deepened the kiss. He claimed her in a soul-deep kiss that fried every coherent thought as though she'd stuck her fingers into a light socket.

He nibbled and sucked her lower lip and ran his tongue along the inside, then kissed her hard and deep again, leaving her senses reeling. Instinct had her trying to put her arms around his neck. Frustration at being bound had her growling low in her throat.

She wanted to run her hands through his gorgeous mane of auburn hair and just plain hold on as his tongue swirled inside her mouth. He alternated by teasing her then claiming her firmly and completely.

Needing to take part, she tried to kiss him back, needed to taste and feel him. As soon as her tongue entered his moist mouth, his lips closed over her and he sucked hard. The erotic kiss slid through her bloodstream like warmed honey, thick and sweet. His kisses were richer than the creamiest chocolate, headier than a glass of good champagne, and sweeter than a rose in full bloom. Her head spun as though she'd drunk too much bubbly, yet it wasn't enough.

She wanted—needed—more. Leaning into him, supported and held by his arms, desire left Caitie overwhelmed. She'd never considered herself a good kisser, had often wished that part of the mating game could be skipped, but kissing this man was like finding money hidden in an old purse— surprise, excitement, followed by pure pleasure with the newly discovered windfall. His expertise and her response was her windfall.

He shifted her in his arms, the movement parting his vest. One of her breasts slid across his hard, warm chest. His thick mat of hair cushioned and teased her sensitive nipple. She groaned, the sound a throaty purr. Blood pounded in her ears and raged through her body as though a flash flood had had swept through her, and each breath became a shallow pant.

More. She wanted everything this man had to give, and as she was a greedy little bitch, she demanded more. *Hot damn.* If he was this good with his mouth, with what she usually regarded as a boring kiss from any of her previous lovers, then she was in for one hell of a ride.

She thrust her hips out, seeking, needing, and demanding and whimpered when his erection brushed her belly. Excitement vibrated through her. Her clit throbbed and pulsed as though electrical impulses were being fired into her. She squeezed her legs tight, trying to hold those sensations inside. She groaned as the pressure shot desire outward from her center.

"Spread your legs." The deep baritone of his voice turned her knees weak.

She obeyed. He shoved one thigh between hers and lifted. She cried out as leather scraped across her heated core.

"What do you want?" Damon trailed his lips along her jawline.

"You. Inside." She panted. A sharp tug to her hair made her wince and add a hasty "Sir."

"You want my cock buried deep inside your pussy?" He rubbed his chest against her straining breasts.

Damn. His voice, the frank talk, his teasing of her breasts, and the pressure of his thigh against her sex turned her insides to mush. "Yes, Sir. Please, Sir, fuck me." She flushed, embarrassed to be so desperate, but she'd beg if he demanded.

Damon lifted his head and held her gaze. "Tell me, my sweet Belle, if given a choice, would you experience your first orgasm right now, hard and fast while riding me. Or would you rather make this moment last, wait until you're screaming and begging for me to allow you to come." He pressed his thigh high, his large hands smoothing over her back until he reached the swell of her ass. His fingers curved and gripped her globes, urging her into a slow, easy, rocking rhythm.

Oh, my god. How could she choose? Explosions of pure lust racked her body, which made thinking impossible. The thought of his taking her right now sent her heart thumping against her ribs. Blood pounded in her ears, and need coiled deep inside her pussy. She bucked against him, wanting that first delicious orgasm yet the idea of him driving her mad, making her beg and scream, buckled her legs. She'd never even come close to needing a man to that degree.

"Hard and fast," she whimpered, thrusting her hips back and forth, feeling the sweet rise toward that coveted peak. She needed to come now. There'd be more, lots more. Candy at Halloween. He could drive her wild next time.

He laughed low in his throat, his breath tickling her nose. His lips brushed hers. "Where's your sense of adventure, little sub?"

"You're a stranger," she gasped, tilting her head back, giving him access to her mouth. Damn, but she wanted her hands free so she could hold this man. "This is very adventurous for me." She yearned to run her fingers across his chest and follow that arrow of dark hair down, down, down to where his cock lay hidden and out of sight.

"By the end of tonight, we won't be strangers, my sweet Belle." He rocked her harder, faster.

Close. So close. She clenched her muscles, readied herself for that final thrust that would send her spiraling out of control. His leg lowered, the pressure eased.

"More. Now!" The words burst from her, a cross between a wail and demand.

He released her and stepped away.

Shock trembled through her at the abrupt halt.

She'd been on the verge of coming. Her body ached to the point of pain. "God, no. Don't stop."

Without his warm thigh pressed against her, the air felt cold against the wetness on the inside of her thighs and higher. Instinctively, she tried to grab him and yank him back to her. She stumbled, forgetting her cuffed wrists.

Off balance, she'd have fallen had Damon not caught and steadied her. A frustrated moan escaped, even as she was grateful he didn't let her fall flat on her face.

He gripped her chin with his thumb and forefinger. "Rule one once again. Subs don't demand. You may ask or beg."

Dazed by the raging need running through her, Caitie blinked in confusion. "Your fault. How can I think when you're driving me crazy?" She couldn't help the thread of sulk in her voice. No one else had ever left her feeling so vulnerable. She'd had more wham-bam-thank-you-ma'am fucks than she cared to admit.

Damon did not fall into the selfish, rutting pig category. She had no doubt he'd satisfy her in a way she'd never experienced, and she wasn't sure that was a good thing after all. Her body and mind sensed there was more to him, that perhaps by the end of their weekend, it wouldn't be so simple to walk away. She'd certainly never forget him and was willing to bet, even though she hadn't had him yet, she'd never find another lover quite like Damon the Dom.

He ran the pad of his thumb across her bottom lip. "That's the point, little sub. You're not supposed to think. Just feel."

Damn. She was feeling, lots of feeling going on inside her, including feeling edgy and out of control. She glared at him. "You gave me a choice."

He smiled. "I said *if* given a choice. The decision is ultimately mine to make."

"That's not fair." God, her body was a mass of tingling nerves, and her mind raw with need. How much teasing could she bear? Was this to prove he was in charge and held all the power? Dammit, if it was, it was working. Without her hands, she was helpless, had to rely on him to ease the ache he'd created.

"Nice to know I have such an effect." He kissed her hard.

When he lifted his head, Caitie's world was once again spiraling out of control. He slid his arms around her and unsnapped the clasp holding the cuffs together. "Rule two. Subs may only come when Doms give permission."

"What?" She gulped. "Um, Sir, you cannot be serious." Was he crazy? If he touched her again, stroked his thigh against her or used his fingers–please let him use his fingers–there'd be no way in hell she could *not* come.

"If you come without permission, you'll be punished."

Punished? There was that word again. Caitie chewed her lower lip, worried about what that meant, but with her hands free, she made no comment. Instead, she held out her arms.

When he lifted a brow, she rolled her eyes. "Please, Sir. Could you remove the handcuffs?"

The silver of his eyes gleamed like mercury. "Why are you cuffed?"

She frowned. "I don't know. *Sir*. I assumed it was part of the game. I was being treated like a prisoner taken to the dungeon—to my beast."

"I ordered them. You'll find I have a reason for everything I do or ask. In this case, the cuffs are your first lesson in learning what it means to be submissive and giving total control to your Dom." He lifted a brow. "You haven't learned it, so they stay on."

Caitlin blinked back tears of frustration. She was so confused, so achy, and so needy. "Maybe this isn't going to work. I'm not a doormat," she said, her voice low with regret. She didn't want to leave, needed this man to finish what he'd started, but she was used to giving the orders and looking out for those in her life. When she wanted something, she went after it. Waiting and patience weren't her strongest virtues.

To her surprise, Damon grinned and drew her close, the backs of his fingers lifting her chin. "A sub is not a doormat, which proves you don't understand the concept of a power exchange. Let's go on to lesson two."

She felt like a ping-pong ball, bounced from one emotion to another. Part of her was relieved he didn't send her packing, yet she was also afraid he'd end up disappointed in her. She clearly did not get the rules between Doms and subs or, shit, even what made a good sub. All she had to do was keep her mouth shut and obey, and so far, she, who seldom failed at any task she undertook, had failed miserably.

"What is lesson two, Sir?" She tried her best to be meek.

"Practicing rule two." He stepped back and removed his vest and G-string.

Her jaw dropped at the sight of his cock, and the spit in her mouth dried to dust. The man was huge, a stallion among men. Caitie's legs shook. She wanted nothing more than to drop to her knees, take him in hand, and tame his beast.

"Oh, please, Sir." She reached out to stroke him.

He stopped her. "Subs are not allowed to touch without permission. Consider that rule three."

Frustrated, finding all these rules totally unfair, she glared at him. "Just what the hell can subs do? *Sir?*"

He lifted a brow, reminding her he was in charge. "What they are told to do, when they are told to do it, and how they are told to do it," he replied in a firm, almost harsh tone.

Faced with his displeasure, she gulped. Good heavens. She needed a zipper for her mouth. *Submissive, Caitie girl. Remember the candy. Lots and lots of candy.* She bent her head, hoping to appear properly contrite even as her gaze remained fastened on his prime penis.

"Yes, Sir," she said as she eyed his flared mushroomed head, yearned to lick that drop of pre-cum, wrap her hand around him, and lick him like a prized sucker. God, rules were hell, but now that he'd revealed his cock in all its erect glory, nothing else mattered but getting him inside her.

"Remove your dress." He planted his feet apart and stood with his hands behind his back like a soldier at rest.

Caitie didn't hesitate. She had a good body, worked to keep it toned and in shape. While she often wished her boobs weren't quite so generous, she now was glad, as he'd made it clear he found them desirable. She untied the apron. It fell to the carpet. Staring into his silvery-blue eyes, she pulled her dress up and over her head, taking her time, teasing him as he'd tormented her. The dress joined her apron, and she stood naked and proud.

Damon sucked in his breath. His balls shot up as though they were puppets on wires. The air whooshed from his lungs. He stepped close, and she slid her fingers over his chest, tunneling through the mat of hair, leaving trails of tingling heat in their wake. He snagged her wrists, clipped them back together, lifted them above her head, and hooked them to a chain woven among the ivy of the fake plant.

Caitlin blinked in dismay and yanked her arms. She cried out. "No. R–"

Damon kissed her hard and deep, in part to stop her from using her safeword and partly to show her she had nothing to fear. He didn't want to break her or push her to the point where she gave up and left.

Normally, if a woman didn't work out as a sub, he'd end the session and save them both the time and effort and spent emotion. Sessions were draining, not only physically but also mentally and emotionally, and he didn't waste his on women who didn't know the score or were unsuited to the lifestyle.

But Caitlin was different, and he couldn't chance her changing her mind. Not yet. He needed her unlike he'd ever needed or wanted anyone else. For three weeks, he'd thought of her, of this weekend and claiming her. Since seeing her photos, she'd haunted his dreams, leaving him aching and on edge. He needed her in a way that both thrilled and scared him. His hands roamed her body, following the sweet curves of her waist and hips, his palms gliding over her soft skin and around to her back to dip over the swell of her ass. He pulled her close, sandwiched his cock against her belly and rubbed.

Her throaty moans reassured him that her moment of panic was past. He lifted his head, stared into her eyes, noting the warring emotions. His fingers dug into her twin cheeks. "Good, Belle," he murmured when she gave no further protest. "I think you've earned a reward."

"My hands?" Her voice was shaky yet hopeful.

He grinned. "I was thinking of my mouth." He dropped slowly and carefully to his knees. The leather scraped against his scarred thigh. He shoved the pain aside and urged her feet apart. Inches from her crotch, he inhaled the musky scent of her arousal and stared at her glistening dark curls that hid the treasure he sought. A glimmer of pink teased and tantalized. His hands skimmed along the insides of her thighs, his fingers brushing over her mound of thick, springy dark hair as he framed her sex and peeled her open as though she were a precious gift.

He lost himself in the view of Caitlin's slick

pussy. She was wet, her clit swollen and peeping from its protective hood. He scraped the pad of his finger across that sensitive nub.

She sucked in air and thrust her hips forward. Damon, unable to resist, touched his tongue to her. He breathed in her warmth, and the taste of her cream exploded in his mouth. His intent to tease her fled beneath the raging need coiling inside him. He licked between her swollen lips and didn't stop until he reached the grand prize.

Gripping her hips, he circled that sweet nub as though it were a tasty treat he planned to enjoy for a long time, but after two slow, lazy licks, he closed his mouth over her clit and sucked hard and deep.

She bucked and screamed his name. His balls tightened and jumped once more. His cock throbbed, the blood flow making him bob like a buoy in the ocean. In his ears, the roar of lust rose and merged with her whimpers and cries, forming a chorus of melodies and harmonies.

Caitlin's hips circled, thrust, and demanded. Damon lifted his head and dipped his thumb inside her pussy. She was wet, and when she contracted her muscles, she drew him into her moist sheath. He withdrew his thumb and eased two fingers inside. She moaned, and her body pulsed and coated him with womanly juices.

He loved how easily she responded, how she put her trust in him. His gut clenched at the sight of his fingers sliding into her hot pussy, and the way she contracted around him left him breathless. She protested when he stopped.

"Look at me," he ordered.

Her eyes were smoky with passion, her features contorted in a mask somewhere between pain and pleasure as he plunged deep. He rotated between slow teasing strokes and fast, furious pumps.

She threw her head back and cried out. Her breathy mews continued, broken by an occasional gasp, moan, or harsh scream as he fucked her. She whimpered and begged.

Not enough. Blind need. For him. He needed that from his sweet Belle.

Sweat gathered and pooled at the base of his spine. Need churned in his balls. The pain of denial left him breathless. He yearned to shove his cock deep into her slick pussy, feel her tight sheath fist him, squeeze, and take from him as much as he planned to take from her.

Tipping his head back, he delved between her moist lips. She was liquid satin. He circled and rubbed her clit with the tip of his tongue.

Caitie's knees shook as intense need flooded her body. He fucked her hard and deep, sending her higher and farther. He teased and taunted, made her feel incredibly sexy and desirable. She thrust out her hips, demanding more. God, she wanted him to suck her again, needed those clever lips on her, squeezing her clit and sucking her until he sent her over the edge.

She whimpered and tried to grab onto that all-consuming need, tried to hold it, tame it, control it, center it, but desire raged inside her like a beast let loose to ravage the land. A thick, swirling fog blinded her, dampened all sound but the pounding of her heart and the rush of blood racing through her veins. The blanket of white was everywhere yet insubstantial. Nothing mattered except the glorious waves of pure pleasure consuming her.

His tongue flicked across her clit, the tip probing one moment, then tracing circles around that part of her that was desperate to find release. She threw her head back and sagged as her knees buckled. She bucked wildly. "Yes. Oh, my god, yes," she yelled, eager to gather herself in and let go.

His thumb replaced his tongue and flicked across her clit. "Do not come until I say."

His voice shattered the haze of blinding desire though she found it hard to focus or think with his fingers pumping in and out of her. Sucking in her breath, Caitie knew if he kept that up she'd come with or without permission. "Yes, Sir."

God, don't let her blow it and make him stop. Heat and need consumed her. Her vision narrowed. There was only him and her and the magic of touch.

He fell into a hard, fast rhythm. She shuddered. "Please, Sir. I can't wait." Her voice rose.

"Not yet." His thumb pressed firmer, circled faster.

Her body shook and trembled, and she tried to keep from tightening, but like a clock wound to the point of breaking, she was ready to spring apart. She gasped, drew in a deep breath, fought for control. Her cry was thin as her lungs struggled to breathe.

"Now, my sweet sub. Scream for me and come."

Those had to be the sweetest words she'd ever

heard. She didn't need her beast to tell her twice. She let go. She shouted his name and flew, grabbing at the fistfuls of bright, shiny balls of candy flying around her.

Damon tasted and drank her sweet cream as she shuddered and shook. Her pussy clamped on his fingers, and each contraction drew him deeper. She was hot, wet, and her orgasm was the most beautiful gift he'd ever received.

Her cries were music to his ears as she sobbed his name over and over. He gentled his mouth and didn't stop until she sagged, completely spent. Standing, he wrapped his arm around her, taking most of her weight while he unchained her wrists. Her arms fell and draped over his head.

Each breath came in a ragged gasp as her forehead dropped to his shoulder. He held her, loving the way her curves molded against him. His hands closed over her ass, and he lifted her until she stood on her toes. His erection skimmed through her damp curls, seeking entrance to her slick pussy.

Damon wanted nothing more than to lift her into his arms and drive himself deep inside her, but he had plans.

"That was incredible," she breathed.

Her eyes were dark like liquid smoke. "Did you like your reward?"

"Yes." Her voice was a soft purr. "I never knew it could be so intense." Her admission made her blush.

"That was just the beginning." He trailed a finger along her flushed cheek. "The first stop on a Halloween journey filled with as many houses to visit as you can handle."

She smiled shyly. "May I reward you now, Sir Beast?"

"Giving yourself to me is my reward. And that is the center of what we are doing. You weren't sure you liked being bound, but you enjoyed the experience. Correct?"

She frowned but nodded.

"You trusted me, and I took care of you. I pleased you." He waited for her to absorb what he said.

"I liked very much the way you took care of me."

"And that pleases me. That was a power exchange."

"But you—um—you haven't come."

He chuckled. "Trust me, little sub. I plan to fuck you to the moon and back."

Chapter Five

Good god. *Fuck her to the moon and back.* Her insides buzzed in anticipation, and her legs trembled. Most guys, if they got the girl off first wouldn't wait to seek their own satisfaction. The fact that Damon wasn't in a hurry to take care of his needs gave her pause. He'd pleased her more than anyone else, yet it wasn't enough. Deep in her core, desperate need pooled. She should have been satisfied and sated. Instead, her desire for this man had only grown stronger.

"Shall we continue? I believe we have more houses to visit and a lot more candy to gather."

"Yes, Sir," she answered shyly, which, considering everything they'd done, seemed silly.

"Good. Go into the bedroom and position yourself on the bed."

She frowned. Position? She had no idea what he meant, but she was curious to see what he had planned. She turned, spotted the set of double doors, and pushed them open. And came to an abrupt halt.

The bedroom was huge. Her attention focused on the large king-sized bed that took up a third of the space. She spotted a black wedge in the center of the bed. His orders suddenly made sense. Her eyes went wide at the sight of a pair of leather cuffs attached to each side of the wedge. Her heart thumped painfully.

"Was there something in my request you did not understand?"

His deep voice rumbled through her. He was back to full Dom mode. "No, Sir."

"Then I expect you to obey without delay."

Fear warred with need. *Trust. Learning to give up control.* That's what he was addressing in this first session. Damn, she'd wanted a weekend of awesome sex, and so far, from the preview he'd given her, if she did what he asked, she'd get the best sex of her life. So with hesitant steps, she entered the room.

Damon watched her climb on the bed and eye the wedge. With a deep breath, she draped herself over it. He let out his breath, relieved she'd obeyed. More than any other sub, he needed her to trust him and give him control. Each time she did was a gift he treasured.

The mattress dipped beneath his weight as he positioned himself behind her. Was there a sexier sight than a woman's ass in the air, begging to be stroked and all those crevices explored? Not in his mind. He noticed she'd closed her eyes tightly and was chewing her lower lip, a sure sign that she was nervous. Did she expect him to cuff her legs to the wedge?

That had been the plan. Instead, he caressed her back, following the curve of her spine from the nape of her neck to the crease below her ass, his fingers brushing her sex with each pass. "I'm proud of you, Belle. I know this isn't easy, but it'll be worth it."

"It'd better be," she sighed, relaxing.

His palms crested her ass, trailed down her thighs, and eased them apart. "Good Doms reward obedient subs. You did as I asked and earned yourself more candy."

Damon cupped each cheek and lifted, spreading her open. He stared at her weeping pussy. His gut tightened with need, and his cock bobbed and bounced as the blood pounded through his veins. How easy it would be to plunge inside her and give them both what they each wanted and needed.

But he'd told her the truth. He took his responsibilities as a Dom seriously, and though he needed to please her, he was also responsible for teaching her about her own sexuality. And that meant pushing her, experimenting, discovering her boundaries, then allowing her to grow and shine.

She surprised him. For such a confident woman, she was nervous, unsure of herself, and shocked at her own responses. He knew she hated giving up control, yet when she did, she responded so magnificently.

He trailed one finger over her tight rosette, then circled her glistening slit. Her sigh turned to a moan, and she wiggled her hips. He wanted her good and hungry before he got to the next part of his plan. He needed her willing to put her trust in him. So he'd prove himself worthy.

"House number two. Hard and fast, Belle." He eased a finger inside her wet, throbbing sheath and out. She was hot and creamy. Her inner muscles tightened. He let out his breath. Damn, she felt good. *Good hell*. This woman was heaven on earth. His gaze latched onto the rhythmic way her pussy contracted and released. Beneath his palm, the muscles in her ass clenched.

He grinned, thrust two fingers inside, and curved them. Her shriek pleased him more than any words she could have uttered and set off a string of small bombs of pure lust in his balls as cum churned and fought for release. God, at this rate, he was liable to embarrass himself. He couldn't recall the last time he'd come without meaning to.

She moaned. "Please, Sir." She panted the plea, remembering his rule and not wanting him to stop.

"Yes, my sweet, innocent Belle." He pressed her G-spot hard.

A bolt of pleasure flared from pussy to clit. Caitie shrieked his name and exploded like a cannon ball shot high into the heavens. Everything both faded yet became. Her body fell away and she soared high into a world filled with splashes of color weaving into rainbows sparkling stars. She convulsed and jerked, each burst of pleasure sending her higher into that magical place where there was just her and the man who sent her over the edge.

Gasping, she went limp. How was it possible for this orgasm to be better, sweeter, and stronger? She wasn't sure she was still alive. Until he licked her and drank her cream. His finger slipped into her folds and found her clit.

"Again," he murmured.

"Not possible." Yet she was so sensitive, so on edge, his fingers turned her mind to mush and the impossible became so. Her world narrowed to him and how he made her feel, then even that faded as he shot her back up, kept her in that heavenly cloud until she thought all life had fled.

She wasn't sure how long it took for her to become aware of the man behind her. "Oh, god," she gasped. "House number two. A duplex. Jackpot. I think my body is numb. Tell me we aren't done."

His body blanketed hers. He laughed in her ear. "Greedy sub."

"Never had candy so good," she murmured as she sought to calm her racing heart and draw air into her starved lungs. His cock rubbed her ass, the thick head nudging her slit, searching for entrance. She tilted her hips up. God, she needed that huge shaft inside her, filling her, sending her back into a world where nothing else mattered but the two of them.

His fingers threaded with hers. "What do you want now?"

"Your cock."

He kissed the side of her neck and trailed his lips across her shoulders. He nipped her lightly. "You have to earn it."

"How, Sir?"

"By trusting me." He licked the swirls of her ear, then his weight was gone. She bit her lip to keep from protesting. The mattress shifted, and his arms wrapped around her waist, lifting her. He swept the wedge onto the floor.

"On your back." His warm breath sent shivers through her.

More than eager, she lowered herself, then rolled over to stare into glittering eyes that reminded her of an Alaskan night sky filled with stars—deep and mysterious. He left the bed, opened the drawer in the bedside table, and fished out another pair of cuffs.

Caitie swallowed hard when he held out a hand for her foot. Control. Trust. Damon expected both.

She wrinkled her nose but lifted her right foot. Her heart hammered when he snapped the cuff on, then strode to the other side and cuffed her left ankle.

He sat on the edge of the bed. "Very good."

With a gentle nudge, he pushed her feet close to her thighs then urged her knees to butterfly open. His gaze latched onto her. The heat smoldering in his eyes warmed her. She licked her lower lip, wondering if he would use his mouth again or, if this time, he planned to fuck her with his cock.

He grabbed a leather cuff from beneath the bed, and before she knew what he intended, he'd fastened it around one thigh, then snapped it to her ankle cuff. Once more, panic hit when she realized he was going to truss her up like a calf being branded.

He shifted to the other side of the bed and lifted a second restraint.

"Wait." Her voice sounded high and reedy.

His brows rose.

She drew in a deep breath. *Control. Give him what he wants. Needs. And he'll give you what you want. Need.* The point of the weekend was to experience and discover new possibilities. Hadn't she decided to participate in this event because she found sex boring and unsatisfying? She breathed, counted to ten, and then nodded. She resisted the urge to close her eyes.

Her heart pounded as he fastened the second cuff and ankle and then connected the chains of both. She was flat on her back, wide open and totally helpless and... *Shit*. He was free to do whatever he wanted. A delicious shiver ran though her. *Pleasure me. Take me. Make me yours.* It shocked her to realize how much she needed him to do just that.

Another dip into the drawer had her worried. She relaxed when he pulled out a foil packet. Her mouth watered when he rolled the condom down his rock-hard cock.

At last. Hurry, hurry, hurry. But she was wise enough to hold her demands inside. No way was she going to say something wrong and stop whatever was about to happen. She was ready for house number four.

He climbed onto the bed and ran his palms up along her inner thighs. "Beautiful, little sub." He leaned over, squeezed her breast, and drew the puckered peak into his warm, moist mouth.

His intense sucking sent an electrical zing from nipple to clit. His other hand played with her other breast, rubbing and rolling the tight little bud between his fingers. He alternated between licking and laving one round globe, then the other until she was a mass of agonizing need.

He skimmed her belly. She quivered, waited, yearned for him to touch her clit. It surprised her that she found it strangely erotic to be open, exposed, and bound, totally trapped and at his mercy.

He rose onto his knees. "Ready for more candy?"

He knelt between her legs. Wearing only the black leather chaps, Damon took her breath away. He was rough and rugged, yet gentle. His wide chest, the rich, mat of hair that glinted with red combined with a rock-hard belly made him one hell of a hunk.

She lowered her gaze, feasted on the triangle of curls surrounding his cock like ferns uncurling at the base of a tall redwood. His erection throbbed, the crown swollen and gloriously purple with the blood surging through his veins. Make that one hell of a *sexy* hunk.

"Yes, Sir." She licked her lips.

He held out his hand. "First your hands."

Her gaze locked onto his. "What?"

"I'm taking all control from you and in return, I'll give you everything, even more than you ever thought possible."

"But—" She was already trussed and helpless. Wasn't that enough? She couldn't let him take away what little control she had left.

"Do you trust me?" His voice was low, calm.

Her protest died. Desire glowed in his eyes. Though he kept his features schooled, she read how much he needed her to accept him and freely take what he offered.

"Yes or no," he asked again.

She answered truthfully. "Yes." She sounded hesitant and unsure, but she held out her bound hands.

He unhooked them, and one at a time, snapped

them to her thighs. The moment he rose onto his knees, she realized just how vulnerable, how helpless she was. This man was a stranger. It didn't matter that he'd given her three mind-blowing orgasms. He was free to do whatever he wanted, and she couldn't stop him.

She was scared. She couldn't move. All choice, all control was gone. "I changed my mind." Blind panic raced through her. She struggled to free herself, to breathe, but her chest felt as though an elephant sat on her.

Damon leaned over and framed her face between his hands. "Easy, little sub. You're not helpless. You have your safeword. You hold all the power now."

His words, his low voice broke through the cloud of fear. *Safeword. Red.*

She opened her mouth to use it then frowned. "Say that again?" How could she have power when she couldn't even scratch an itch on her nose or ass?

"If you accept this, you are handing me power and control."

"That makes sense. You hold the power, not me." Tears threatened. She didn't want to fail or come across cowardly, but this was too much.

He thumbed away the single tear. "The power is yours. Your choice to keep or give. By giving control, you have the power because you can take it back anytime. I only receive it when you agree to give it or share it with me and only for as long as you wish." He kissed her lightly. "This, if you choose to think of it as such, is your gift to me, one I'll treasure always."

His words stilled and calmed her, and she recalled his explanation of what he called a power exchange. When he lifted his head, she stared into his eyes. "This is what you meant by taking control and power?"

His hand covered her mound, his finger resting on her clit. "It's one way, yes."

"And I get—"

His mouth curved. "Candy, my gorgeous sub. Lots of candy." He pinched her swollen nub lightly.

Caitie gasped. She wasn't totally happy, even if she did want more of those fantastic orgasms. "House number four better have some prime goodies."

Chapter Six

Damon chuckled, leaned over, and kissed her hard and deep. "I think house four might have the best treats yet along with some fun games to be played." He saw through her attempt at humor. She was afraid and unhappy with what he asked of her. Her spunk and bravery earned his admiration and made him determined to show her that her trust in him was well placed.

"Maybe I won't play," she muttered. "See how you like them apples."

He cocked one brow. "Excuse me?"

"Oh, sorry. See how you like that. Sir."

Holding her gaze, the combination of rebellion, lust, and fear made him determined to give her the best orgasm yet and prove to her that he'd take care of her every need. He slipped his finger inside her quivering pussy, pulling cream to slick her hard nub. The muscles of her abdomen tightened, but she didn't speak.

Damon couldn't help smiling when he noticed she had her lips firmly clamped shut. His blood quickened. His sub continually surprised and pleased him. He'd been prepared for her to use her safeword and halt their session. And he wouldn't have pushed her. He'd known this might be too much, too soon, but he wanted to see how much control she'd relinquish.

So far, she'd held nothing back, and that thrilled him more than it should. Her trust and willingness to place her well-being in his hands was a gift unlike any other he'd received. Her bravery, even if given unwillingly, earned his respect.

"I promise you'll like what I do to you." He rubbed her clit, loving the feel of her as much as the flash of pleasure in her eyes.

"Maybe I'll just lie here and take it." She swallowed a moan.

Damon laughed. "Ah, a challenge." He understood her perfectly. She'd given him control of her body but not her mind. "Now this is a good game for our Halloween trick or treating theme. Shall we see how long it takes for you to scream and beg?"

He eased his finger through her folds and circled her weeping pussy. She shuddered and couldn't stop from clenching her muscles and jerking her hips upward, but she remained stubbornly silent.

Unable to resist, he knelt between her legs and fastened his mouth over her clit. Her cry burst out of her and sent a jolt through his balls and into the tip of his cock. *Fuck*. He might be pushing her to her limits, but she'd shoved him well past his. He sucked and licked, drove her hard and fast. Her clit swelled, and her whimpers were music to his ears.

"Ready to beg?" He flicked his tongue back and forth.

"No." Her voice sounded strained as she pulled at her hands.

He lifted his head. "Not bad. Pretty good control. Let's try this." He thrust his middle finger deep inside her quivering pussy. She gasped and whimpered. He stroked her slow but kept her from cresting.

She arched her head and choked back a cry. Her chest heaved, bringing his gaze to her tits. Each breath sent the pair jiggling. With difficulty, he returned his attention to her face and absorbed every expression, every shudder as he fingerfucked her.

"Bondage is only one form of control, my sweet beginner. This is another. Let's see how controlled you can be." He added a second finger and stroked faster and deeper.

Caitie's breath whooshed out. She rolled her head side to side. Her body was on fire. She ached, and she throbbed like a cat in heat. Holding back the need to come was painful. She tried to keep from crying out, from moaning, but he was taking away her choice. She wanted to cry, yet at the same time, his mastery thrilled her.

"Ready to scream and beg?"

Staring into his eyes, she knew she was fighting a losing battle. Didn't he understand she needed to keep something for herself? "No. Sir. You can. Make me. Can't stop. You." Each word exploded out of her. She'd be damned if she gave him what he wanted. He might control her body, but no man controlled her mind. "I let you—do this. That's. Enough."

"I'll have all of you, little sub. All or nothing."

She fisted her hands and wished she could grab him and force him to take her completely. She couldn't stop from whimpering when he once again found that dime-sized sweet spot inside.

"Cheating," she gasped, trying to hold on to the hair-thin thread of control.

"But you like it. Say you want to come. Beg, sweet Belle." He rolled her clit between his fingers and, at the same time, pressed harder against her G-spot.

The flare of pain combined with pure pleasure set off explosions deep inside. God, who was she kidding? This man could do anything, and she'd let him. Because he was right. Giving up control so far had given her the best sex of her life. Her small act of rebellion fell like the walls of Jericho.

"Yes!" The admission tore from her throat. Her head felt light from lack of air that came from holding her breath and trying not to give in, and her entire body buzzed as though a swarm of bees had flown a path from head to toes. Her emotions were in turmoil, and her control stretched to the breaking point. The beast had tamed Belle.

"I need you. Need to come. Are you happy?" She needed Damon, her Dom, her beast, and the pleasure he gave, even if it meant giving him what he demanded—her all.

"For now, little sub. For now." He removed his fingers and plunged his cock deep into her pussy.

The shock, the thrill of his finally filling her sent her over the edge. Everything around her turned white and silent except for her scream of surrender. She shook and trembled beneath the force of the spasms tearing through her. The spasms went on and on, taking her higher.

Damon leaned over and kissed her gently. By the time she came back to total awareness, her hands, legs and feet were free. Good lord, he'd sent her over the edge just by ramming his cock inside. He hadn't moved and hadn't come. Just filled her and joined them. She panted.

"More," she begged, feeling him throb inside her.

He lifted her legs and draped them over his shoulder. "Look at me, Caitlin." He pulled her hips closer, slid his palms beneath her ass, and lifted.

Caitie couldn't have taken her eyes off him had she tried. His face was taut with tension. Lines bracketed his mouth, his lips compressed from holding himself back. His nostrils flared as he drew in a deep breath. Here was a man in total control, yet she sensed he was about to lose himself in her as much as she'd lost herself in him. The thought thrilled her.

His cock eased out slowly then back in. She pressed her hands into the mattress and just absorbed the feel of him. His first plunge into her pussy was a blur. Her mind had been too overwhelmed with too many sensations to really appreciate how he felt inside her. Though she ached and yearned for more, she focused wholly on him.

He'd pushed her from one end of the emotional spectrum to the other, and now he was joining them, combining their power and pleasure. She'd waited so long for this that she didn't want to miss a single, heart stopping moment.

He glided into her smoothly. His size took her breath away. He stretched her, filled her, and completed her in a way she'd never experienced. "You're so big," she gasped.

"And you're so tight. So fucking hot. I need you, Belle. Take me. Take all of me."

She shivered with pleasure. His steel-hardened shaft fit like the missing puzzle piece. He completed her picture. Her pussy pulsed around his cock. Her inner muscles formed a tight glove over him, claiming him as he claimed her.

As though he was just as overwhelmed, he held himself still, allowed her to absorb the feel of him embedded inside her. Had any other man felt this wonderful, as if he'd come home? She didn't think so. In that moment, the truth hit. He belonged.

If Damon had simply fucked her when she'd entered the room, she wouldn't have this connection with him. It would have been just another fuck—no doubt a good fuck—but no more. The emotional bond he'd forged translated into a much stronger physical bonding.

He lifted her hips. The motion allowed him to go even deeper, and she gasped, barely able to breathe. Blood pounded through her and inside her, his cock throbbed and vibrated with its own suppressed need. And she felt totally and absolutely in control.

"You are mine, Belle. Mine." He leaned over her, his hands on the coverlet beside her face, his mouth hovering over hers.

"Yes, Sir," she panted. And it was true. She needed whatever her weekend beast could give her. She tightened her inner muscles and squeezed. His hiss of breath pleased her, then his mouth claimed hers, his tongue sweeping in. Moaning deep in her throat, she kissed him just as passionately.

Damon was in both heaven and hell. She surrounded him with her moist heat. Every contraction of her pussy felt like dozens of hands stroking his dick. He resisted the urge to pump in and out and send them both reeling. For just this one moment in time, he needed to be one with this woman who both fascinated and mesmerized him.

He tilted his hips, gliding out of her. Her groan mirrored his. He eased back in. She was so tight he was afraid of hurting her. He slid his hand between their bodies. "I want to feel you come with me inside." Needed to feel her consume him before he lost all control. He stroked her swollen clit.

Her cry pleased him, as did the waves of pleasure stroking his cock. He drove her hard and fast. Sweat beaded on the sides of his face and ran down his back. The base of his spine tingled with the need to fuck her until his brains leaked out his ears. "Hurry, Belle."

"Yes," she whimpered and arched beneath him. "Yes. Yes. Yes. God, I'm coming." Her voice rose to a high shriek, and her fingers twisted in the comforter.

He stroked her clit harder and faster until she went stiff and screamed his name. Her pussy convulsed around his cock, and his shout joined her as spasm after spasm threatened to shred the last of his control.

Before her body calmed, he rose back onto his knees, pushed her legs toward her chest, lifting her and staring at their bodies where they were joined.

He pulled out, shuddered with pleasure at the sight of her cream coating his cock, then thrust inside her heavenly warmth. His balls throbbed, his cum churned like a whirlpool threatening to draw in a helpless craft and drown it. If he didn't fuck her hard and fast right now, he'd be the one drowning.

He pumped his hips and fucked her, driving deep with each thrust. Many women couldn't handle his size, but Caitie molded around him as though made for him. Just him.

Her breathy cries turned to whimpers. "So good," she moaned. Her fingers splayed open, clutching and releasing the comforter. "More."

He went deeper, felt her shudder and draw him in, felt her acceptance as she took all of him. And lost control. He loved the way her eyes glazed with passion, with need. For him. Her back arched and she threw her head back, exposing the smooth column of her neck.

Damon filled her, moved as one with her. Caitlin's cries fill the room. She gripped his cock with her pussy. He felt the flare of ecstasy building deep inside her.

His angle and his size allowed him to stroke that sweet spot that he knew would set off mini explosions in her clit. He held her legs firm. She rocked and clenched her muscles, matching his pounding rhythm. "Look at me." She obeyed. Sweat dripped down the sides of his face, and his arms bulged when he dropped onto his hands, his mouth inches from hers. "With me, Caitlin. With me. Say my name when you come. Scream my name."

"Now, Damon. Take me again." She gripped

his shoulders, her fingers trailed down his back, her nails scraping.

He shuddered, and his thrusts turned frantic. Blood pounded in his ears, his groin, and even deep in his wound, the pain adding an edge to the lust driving him to pump harder and faster.

"Damon!" She screamed his name when he plunged harder and faster with the intensity of a man driven over the edge.

"Now. Now. Now." His shouts echoed around her.

She screamed his name over and over as he shot them both high, into a void filled with white heat and sparks of color, their own private firework display.

****

Damon cradled Caitlin in his arms. He'd fallen on the bed, she'd wrapped her arms around him, and in a tangle of arms and legs, he'd drawn her close, pleased when she put her head on his chest and promptly fell asleep. He ran his hand along the curve of her side, dipped into the valley of her waist, and caressed the swell of her hip.

He retraced his movement, finding it soothing to touch her. He envied her ability to sleep so soundly and peacefully. He smiled and brushed his lips across her forehead. Caitlin Olsen was nothing like he'd figured. He'd been prepared for a confident woman, a woman used to being in charge of her life. And he'd gotten that and so much more.

He bit back a chuckle when he remembered how she'd come through the door with fire in her eye and an attitude big as the moon on her shoulders. His first impression had been that they were a bad match, that Bryce and Glorie were wrong in their assessment of her and the weekend would not work out.

It had taken less than ten minutes for her to pique his curiosity. Twenty for him to decide he wanted her at any cost, and now, after two intense hours, he wasn't sure three days would be enough.

She shifted in his arms, sighed in her sleep, and threw one leg over his. He winced at the brief flash of pain that jangled the nerves in his thigh but didn't shift her. He liked having her draped over his body. It'd be so simple to stroke her ass and cup her dark mound. Maybe he'd wake her nice and slow and take them both on a leisurely ride. No, better not. *Let her sleep.* He had a big evening planned.

Drawing her closer, he rubbed his cheek on her silky hair and grinned. She'd lived up to his expectations this afternoon. As a Dom, he'd pushed her hard, intending to break through her need to control. He'd needed to know if she would submit and where her boundaries lay.

And what a surprise he'd received. She challenged him, pushed him to the breaking point all while submitting completely. He'd earned her trust. He couldn't have asked for more, yet he wanted more.

If their earlier session was about control and power, tonight's focus was on getting to know her, learning what she liked, and again, pushing her to see how far she'd go. She was so responsive, he couldn't wait for later. He closed his hand over her breast and flicked his fingers over her nipple until it tightened, then ran his palm over her ass.

She shifted, her knee brushing his hardening cock. Her eyes flew open.

"Ah, you're awake. Can you handle more candy?" He rolled on top of her, snagged her hands, and drew them both over her head.

Smiling, she parted her legs, welcoming him into the cradle of her hips. "No such thing as too much candy."

"Good, let's go see what house five is offering."

"You are mistaken, Sir. I believe we are on number seven. Four was a triplex."

Laughing, Damon slanted his mouth over hers. "You are correct, little sub. House seven it is, and if you are very good, it, too, might end up being a duplex."

Chapter Seven

After a nap, orgasms number seven and eight, followed by a long shower, Caitie was refreshed and energized. She dressed in a clean costume, similar to the one she'd worn when she arrived at Pleasure Manor, but in nutty brown. Alone in the bathroom, she grinned at her reflection. The mansion was aptly named and her friend Maize had not exaggerated when she'd claimed orgasms were handed out like candy at Halloween.

The beginning had been rocky. She'd nearly decided this Dom/sub stuff wasn't her cup of tea, but she was super glad she'd stuck it out. Damon was a sex god. He knew just how to please women—her. She didn't want to think about him with other women. But hey, she'd take the three days with him and be eternally grateful.

And maybe ruined for any other man.

No one else had ever made her feel the way he did. Hell, she hadn't known it could be so damn good. Their last round of lovemaking had been so different. He'd taken his time, sending her over the edge, showing her a gentle, tender side. Number eight had been a slow fuck, with measured thrusts as he kept pace with her until they'd flown apart, their voices mingling, their hands clasped, and their bodies arched together. She'd hit the jackpot with him as her Dom. And lover. Too bad it was only for a few days.

Taking a deep breath, she couldn't help but wonder what he had planned for tonight and tomorrow. Saturday was a spa day and the ball, and Sunday, she'd say goodbye and return to reality.

Leaving her hair loose, she left the bathroom. She found Damon in the sitting room, leaning against the mantle, exactly where he'd stood when she first entered. Her stomach fluttered when she glanced up at the pot of ivy, the hidden chain, then at the carpet. She lifted a brow. The taped X was gone.

"Regrets?" He joined her, stopping a foot away. His voice warmed her.

"None," she answered honestly. How could she regret a single moment or a single orgasm? She let her gaze roam over his bare chest. She was tempted to go to him and run her hands over that wide, hard plane. She had a weakness for broad shoulders and tapered hips. But she wasn't sure if they were back to their weekend roles or not.

Her gaze drifted lower to the pair of leather pants that rode low on his hips. Her brows rose. No crotch again, and this time, instead of a shapeless sack, his cock was encased in a bright purple penis glove. Good grief, the man was hung, a stallion among men.

"Nice," she said, choking as saliva flooded her mouth. And wasn't she just the mare waiting to be mounted. Good grief, sex suddenly consumed her every thought. She blamed her beast for he'd shown her just how sensual a woman she truly was.

Earlier, she'd been too caught up in his demands to appreciate his body. She did so now by walking around him. Her gaze swept across his bare ass, and her heart pattered happily. He had a prime ass—tanned, firm, muscled, and nicely rounded. Yep, a prized stallion and all hers.

"You have a bubble butt," she said, smiling. Her last boyfriend had what she'd termed a baby butt, nothing there to grab onto. Not that he'd been that good a ride that she needed to hang on for dear life. Unlike Damon who was like a scary but exhilarating rollercoaster.

"Am I allowed to touch you?" Her finger itched to explore those firm cheeks and delve into his shadowy crease.

He turned. "Later. We need to get going or we'll be late."

"Where are we going?" She'd assumed they were staying here in their suite of rooms.

"Dinner and a show."

"We're going out?" That was disappointing. She wanted to spend her evening alone with this intriguing man who knew how to stroke her embers to roaring flames, then quench those fires. Realizing his lack of dress meant they weren't leaving the mansion, she was relived.

"Through here." He led her through a hidden door on the far side of the sitting room.

She frowned. He had a slight limp she'd not noticed before. "Wow, a secret passage." The hall was long, narrow with wall sconce's providing light. At the end, he indicated she should go up the stairs. "Oh, what about masks? We're not supposed to leave our rooms without them."

"We have our own area outside. No one will see us."

Caitie stepped out into the late afternoon light. A brick path cut through a walled garden. She spotted benches, a small table, and a cozy swing. A perfectly formed yellow rose lured her in for a sniff. A bed of lavender surrounding a fountain added a sweet fragrance. "I'd love to sit out here. It's beautiful."

He glanced around. "Tomorrow." He grinned. "Got plans for tonight." He led the way along the winding path to a romantically rounded gate framed by an arch of wisteria. Again, she noticed that slight limp. Did he have an injury? Or just pulled a muscle? No, she'd seen brief flashes of pain or discomfort in his eyes, but at the time, her focus had been on what he was doing or what she was feeling.

Thinking back to the darkness and pain she'd sensed buried deep inside the man, she thought perhaps he fit the role of her beast very well indeed. He reminded her of the horses she rescued. Like many, this man had been injured, perhaps mentally as well as physically, and he kept that part of him walled off from the world. She wondered what happened and found she wanted his story.

A horse-drawn buggy awaiting on the other side of the gate put an end to her curiosity for the time being.

Caitie let out a squeal of pleasure. "Is this for us?" She hurried around Damon and through the gate to check out the large chestnut gelding. "What a gorgeous boy." She glanced up. Hastings held the reins. She hid her grin when she thought of her friend having sex with the butler.

"Come, Belle."

Giggling, eager to play along and see what Damon had planned, she curtsied. "Yes, my prince."

Damon lifted a brow. "Prince? I'm a beast, my dearest Belle."

She narrowed her eyes at the thread of harshness in his voice. Yeah, he was, but she saw through his pain and the face he presented to the world to the good man lurking in the shadows. Time perhaps for him to recognize his goodness.

"Nope. The beast is a prince who is cursed. If he learned to love and was loved in return by the age of twenty-one, he'd change back to a prince." She kept it light, not wanting to scare him off or send him deeper into those shadows he tried so hard to hide.

"Then I'm doomed," he sighed.

She cocked her head. "You don't think you'll ever fall in love?"

He chuckled as he helped her into the buggy. "There is that, but the sad fact is, I passed twenty-one a very long time ago."

Caitie laughed. "Did you know that the beast in the movie was never named? It wasn't until a video game and a Broadway musical came along that he was named Prince Adam. According to my research, the animators dubbed him Adam as they needed to call him something besides the Beast while they worked."

"You did research?" Damon slid his arm along

the back of the seat.

She wrinkled her nose. "Not just the movie but the fairytale, though I did watch the DVD. One thing I read when I did an Internet search said they were running short of time while producing the film, so Belle and the Prince's last dance was reused animation from another fairytale production."

"Well, that's cheating."

She grinned at the affronted tone.

The horse's hooves clomped on the gravel path that led into a thick stand of trees. Full sun gave way to muted and dappled light.

When the buggy stopped, Damon stepped out, then, with hands on her waist, lifted her down, letting her body skim over his. He dipped his head and kissed her the minute her feet touched ground. Lost in the feel of his arms around her, and the spicy taste of his mouth on hers, Caitie was barely aware of the horse and buggy continuing onward.

Damon broke the kiss and grinned down at her. "Consider that an appetizer." He took her hand and led her along a narrow path that wound through the woods like ribbon through hair.

The mention of food reminded her of his claim of dinner and a show. "Are we having a picnic?"

He veered off the path, taking a smaller trail. "You could say that. We have our own fine dining establishment upstairs." He pointed.

"Upstairs?" Her jaw dropped. Spread out before them was a large stand of tall, thick-trunked trees with a huge house nestled among trunks and branches.

"You're shitting me!" She recalled Bobby

Betts, the kid next door and how his dad had built a tree house in their backyard but compared to this...his had been a tree shack.

The house sprawled and encompassed several trees and had to be two stories high. With stained wood and gleaming windows—windows in a tree house?—it looked like a miniature mansion.

Rays of sunlight speared through the leaves and sparked off the glass like light bouncing off a large diamond ring. A circular staircase wrapped around the first trunk, leading up into the branches.

"How cool is this? Can we go up?"

Damon motioned her forward. "Dinner awaits."

She paused on the second step and glanced over her shoulder. "And dessert?" She grinned as she continued up the winding stairs. "Always wanted a tree house as a kid, a place to just run and hide and escape with a book and maybe my music."

The wistful thread in Caitlin's voice reminded Damon that she'd assumed the responsibility of an adult at a young age and, most likely, had missed out on many childish delights, while he, as a child, ran wild, having far too many adventures. Many with the law when he reached his teens.

He'd wanted parents who would love him and want him for himself and not the income he provided while she'd became both mother and father to her siblings and caretaker for her mother. Neither of them had had a carefree, happy childhood. He watched her climb and sucked in his breath as she got higher and he caught teasing glimpses of her bare ass and her pink pussy.

Need hummed through him, tempered with a

dull ache. He absently rubbed his thigh. By not allowing himself to limp and show his weakness, the muscles were tight to the point of screaming.

Pulling on his military training, he blocked the pain and continued his climb. She waited for him in front of a fancy, glass door framed in wood. His leg buckled. He caught himself, grateful she had her back to him.

"This is so awesome. I've seen some great tree houses on the net, some big and elaborate enough to almost be a home, but I figured they were just pictures and not real."

Damon opened the door, and she rushed in. He leaned on the doorframe and watched her hurry from one window to another, from the main room to a small sleeping area and even the small corner kitchenette. She climbed a ladder leading up into the loft, came down, and stared up at the skylight above the full size bed.

Moving cautiously, he found a panel of switches and pressed a button. The skylight slid open.

She squealed in delight. "Please tell me we're going to spend the entire night here."

"If you wish."

"Oh, I wish. It's like the inside of an RV but better. It is safe, isn't it? A big wind or earthquake won't topple us.

"It's safe. Bryce paid more for this tiny house than what many pay for a two thousand square foot home." Pride laced his voice. He'd been the contractor, drawn up the plans after consulting several arborists, and had done most of the interior woodwork himself.

He'd been Bryce's pity project. Give the wounded war hero a job that would keep him busy for a long time, so he didn't take his own life. It had worked. He'd poured his heart and soul into this place, and in that sense, it was his.

"Dinner first, then dessert." He wagged his brows. "More houses to go before the night is done, my lovely Belle."

She eyed his crotch and grinned impishly. "Nothing says we can't have dessert first."

Damon laughed. "Behave. You've had enough sweets for a while."

"Never have too many," she said primly as she peered into one wicker basket. "But I suppose you're right. I found dinner, and a good thing. I'm starved. Need protein," she announced.

"Let's eat on the deck. You bring the baskets. I'll grab a quilt and some pillows."

They dished up, passing containers of fried chicken, potato salad, and a basket of fresh baked rolls. She sat with her legs crossed, her dress revealing lots of thigh. He stretched out his bad leg. "So, you own a ranch?"

As much as he wanted to continue her lessons or, hell, just go trick or treating with her, he needed her rested for the evening. Besides, he was curious about her, which was odd, as he never got involved in the lives of his subs.

"Yep. Horse ranch. For the Love of Horses. After my mom died, I took my share of the life insurance and bought a run-down house on a nice bit of land. My younger sister had a horse that we boarded out. It had been abused. I saw how, with a lot of love and care, the animal became loving and trusting in return. Shilo gave me the inspiration to start a horse rescue business. I got some funding, fixed the house, built a couple of barns as the one on the property is about to collapse, then started rescuing neglected and abused horses along with those that are abandoned." She attacked her chicken leg as though she hadn't eaten in days.

Abandoned. His gut clenched at the word, and he shoved his plate aside. His heart pounded, and his throat closed up. God, no panic attacks. Not now. Not around Caitlin. He couldn't show any weakness.

He forced back the darkness creeping across his mind. Focus on her, how the rays of sun fall on her, how they shine on her hair, revealing shades of blonde and red, light and dark browns even golden tones. His gaze dipped to her aged-whisky-colored eyes, then her full lips.

She frowned when she caught him staring and narrowed her gaze. "Hey, are you okay?"

He gulped in air. "I'm fine. Good food, a beautiful woman, what more can a fella want?" He forced lightness and humor into his voice though he felt achingly cold inside.

She studied him. "You looked lost and in pain."

It didn't surprise him that she saw more than he'd like. Hadn't he sensed that aspect of her when he'd first seen the picture of her on horseback? Instead of brushing her off, he shrugged. "We all have our demons, Belle." He used the name deliberately to get things back to the business at hand.

Caitie shook her head. "Don't think I can't see what you're doing, Sir. You're trying to put distance between us." She used her softest voice, as though speaking to one of her spooked horses. She'd seen the despair, hell, she'd felt it, followed by a sense of utter hopelessness and pain, and wondered about his demons. And though he hid it well, she'd spotted his faint limp again and knew his leg caused him pain.

From his demeanor, the way he stood and often acted, she'd bet he'd been in the military as she had several ranch hands who were ex-military and they were as damaged as her horses. As damaged as this man. The thought struck, both physically and emotionally.

She didn't question her instincts. He hid his pain well, but it was there. Her heart went out to him, but he didn't need pity or useless and empty words. "I'm a good listener, Damon."

Damon set his plate aside. "Thanks, but we don't have time for a therapy session. The Beast and his lovely Belle have a show to attend." He stood.

Caitie gathered their plates and stacked them inside one of the wicker baskets. "What do we do with all this?"

"Leave them. They'll be taken care of." He held out his hand and led her to the edge of the deck where a rope and plank bridge spanned the space from the house to another tree. With dusk falling, lights flickered in the branches, and ropes of light lined the bridge. She pressed her hand to her stomach. "You know, I'm not real fond of bridges that sway and move."

Damon drew her close and kissed her long and deep. "It's safe."

Heat settled in her center. It amazed her that one kiss from this man could send her heart racing. She who seldom got turned on by a kiss. "How about we just stay here?"

He grinned. "Nope. Trust the builders. Now, out you go."

The tree house had some sway, but it was gentle, almost like being out on the ocean on a cruise liner in calm seas. She stepped out and crossed quickly until she stood on an octagon platform with a turret roof. An egg shaped chair hung from the ceiling. Another bridge led to a second platform. She groaned.

"Perhaps you can go first. *Sir*. Maybe if I stare at your manly ass, I won't think about the walkways falling apart and hurling me to my death."

He roared with laughter. "Fine. But if you are not right behind me, I'll come back and toss you over my shoulder." He crossed, and again, she noticed he favored one leg. Holding onto the rope rail on the sides, she kept her gaze on his very sexy, very manly ass. The bridge swayed and bounced.

"One more." He pointed.

"Good grief. It's a maze up here." She vowed to explore this wonderland before leaving. She led the way and stood on another platform, this one with a hammock big enough for two. All around them, small outdoor lights twinkled in the trees turning everything into a surreal, fairytale. She could only imagine what the tree would look like once it was full dark.

She grinned. "This is like an amusement park, but better as there aren't a bunch of people behind and in front of you. Now what?"

"Down there." Damon pointed to a plank path much like the circular staircase that wound gently down to another platform. This one appeared to be the end of the sprawling treehouse and contained many spots to sit and enjoy nature.

It too was an octagon but larger with a waist-high railing, a balcony among the leaves and branches. Sheer, white netting hung from the branches. The result reminded her of a cloud or fog drifting through the tree. Caitie stepped inside, and her heart went to mush.

Bench seating lined all but two sides and above her head, more lights twinkled, like fireflies or winking stars. "Magical," she breathed.

"You like it?"

"I *love* it."

"I'm glad. It's mine."

"When you're here, or do you own part of this place?"

"I designed it and my company built it."

Caitie's jaw dropped. "You, Sir, are a freaking genius." She spun around in a circle, amazed and impressed. "It's so clean and fresh. I'd worry about everything getting dirty."

"I had it set up yesterday." He wrapped her in his arms and lowered his head. His lips and tongue trailed along her jawline, then traced a path down her throat. Did he feel the frantic beat of her pulse? "Time to get ready for the show."

"We have to leave already? We just got here."

He laughed. "This, my sweet, is our box seat." He led her to the opening on the other side of the area, waved aside the netting, and stretched out his arms. "There is our stage."

Caitie glanced down. Light was fading, but she could still see. From their height, she spotted a lit path exiting the woods and stretching out into a cleared area surrounded by trees and shrubs. Small, round lamps were planted like flowers around the tiny clearing, forming a nearly perfect circle.

The bushes among the trees were shaped into formal arches, spaced equal distance on each side of the nature-formed stage. Each one had a narrow path lined with lights that meandered into the woods. From her vantage point, the stage resembled a wheel with spokes of light.

"A show down there?" She frowned. "Are we going to be able to see?

"Just wait." Damon opened the seat closest to them and pulled out a box. "Time to get ready.

Caitie peered into the box when he lifted the lid. "Holy cow!"

She stared at a large, pink vibrator with bunny ears and a couple of small devices she wasn't sure what they were. She picked up what looked like a purple dildo but with graduated knobs, starting with a small bead at the top and each one below slightly larger. Each bead was spaced equal distance down a thin rod. It didn't look like a substitute cock.

She touched the small bead the size of her little fingertip. There were five total. "What is this?"

Grinning, Damon took it from her, fisted his

hand around it and pushed and pulled it in and out of his fist. "Vibrating pleasure beads. For back door play."

"Back door—" Her cheeks grew warm. And wetness gathered between her legs as he mimed its use. The beads seemed to pop out of the opening of his fist. "Um, ah, got it." Good lord, she could almost feel it slipping and sliding into her back there.

She turned her gaze to the pink gel vibrator. Her heartrate went through the roof, and she swore she felt it humming inside her already. "That one I know."

Damon chuckled, picked it up, and turned it on. It thrust up and down, and what looked like two little feelers vibrated happily.

"Oh, my." Damn, she was hot and wet and ready for more candy. She touched another toy, this one a stubby, black dildo. She held it up. "A bit on the short side?" It looked like a big, fat, ugly pacifier for a calf or colt. Moisture dampened her thighs at the thought of trying out these sex toys.

Laughing, Damon shook his head. "You are a surprise, my innocent, lovely Belle. That is a butt plug." He reached down, slipped his finger into a small gel-like object with lots of tiny nubs, and pushed a button.

Caitie heard the faint vibration. "You're kidding." Good lord almighty, her clit just swelled in anticipation.

Damon smiled, ran the vibrator along her collarbone. "Shall I demonstrate?"

She sucked in air that immediately whooshed

out. Oh, she wanted that little toy right on her clit. Her heart hammered and need slammed into her center. "I think I understand perfectly what that does." Her voice rose, then muffled as he claimed her mouth in a long, hard, deep kiss.

He broke the kiss, his eyes dark as the last of the sun's rays faded. "We'll save this one." He fisted his fingers in her skirt and drew her dress over her head. "Game on, sweet."

Caitie gulped. She was out in the open. Well, there was netting everywhere around her except right in front.

"Yes, Sir," she said and hoped no one walking below glanced up.

Damon held up the beaded toy. "I think we'll start with this."

Biting her lower lip, eager to try it yet nervous, she wrinkled her nose. "I've never done anything like this." She indicated all the toys in the box.

"You'll trust me to take care of you and give you pleasure?"

How could she not? Everything he'd done had been incredible. She nodded. "Yes, Sir."

Chapter Eight

The light in her eyes and the way she kept licking her lower lip told Damon she was turned on and eager. "Good. Hands and knees then. Face front."

She obeyed, and he slid a pillow beneath her arms and urged her lower. *Fuck.* The sight of her sweet ass in the air had his balls tightening painfully. She wasn't tall and rail thin like a model or a fragile petite doll he'd be afraid to touch in case he was too rough. Nor was she what he thought of as short and curvy.

She had what he considered a very earthy body, reminiscent of old paintings of a different time when women had meat on their bones. His hands skimmed over her frame, her curves, firm muscles, and lots of smooth, silky flesh.

She was strong physically, more than a little stubborn, and had a very adventurous nature. So far, she'd been everything he could have asked for in a partner and more. He ran his hand up the slope of her back, over the crest of her sexy ass, and then to her mound, trailing his fingers through her curls and into the valley of her slick flesh.

She shivered with pleasure, and he wished he still wore that tiny, lovely finger vibrator. He stroked her clit until she moaned and wiggled her hips, then he ran his finger around her slit, finding her wet and slick.

With both hands on her ass, he parted her cheeks and circled her tightly closed rosette with his finger. Grabbing his tube, he squirted a generous dollop of lubricant onto her. Like a prayer plant shrinking from touch, she jerked, the muscles of her sphincter contracting.

"That's cold." Her voice wavered with nerves.

"Have you had anal sex?" He took his time, rubbing and stroking, letting her get used to his touch. He knew the answer from her questionnaire but wanted to engage her. Listening to her answers, her tone, would warn him if she was nervous, scared, or in pain. He was determined that her first experience with back door play be pleasant and positive.

"Nope. No one I trusted enough. Besides, heard too many women say it hurt and was only good for the guy."

"Not true." He circled, then eased the tip of his finger inside, spreading lubricant past the tight ring of muscle. "There are lots of nerve endings back here, and when coaxed properly, they provide a rush of incredible pleasure."

"No shit," she moaned low in her throat. "Feels good."

"We'll go slowly." He stretched her, watching and listening to her breathe. He heard her quick indrawn breath, felt her tense.

"Not too sure about your ass—haha—ssessment," she panted.

He chuckled and after giving her time to adjust

and waiting until she moaned in pleasure and acceptance, added a second finger. The ring of muscle clamped around his fingers and drove the blood from his head to his cock. He was rock-hard and wanted to fuck her ass, but she was so tight and he was so big. "Do you trust me, Caitlin?" Whenever he used her name, she tended to calm.

"Yes, I trust you, Sir."

He was pleased when she fell back into the Dom/sub roles. He added more lube and continued to stroke and stretch her until she relaxed and accepted him. Her breathy pants tempted him to replace his fingers with his cock. God, he wanted to feel her squeeze him until he broke out in a sweat and shouted his triumph, but this time was for her. New experiences, new discoveries.

When he deemed her ready, he held her cheeks open with one hand while easing the small, beaded tip of the anal toy into the center of her rosette. It entered as easily as his fingertip.

She moaned, tipped her hips higher, and he slid the second knob inside. His gut clenched hard, driving the breath from his lungs. "Tell me what you feel, Belle." He was as horny as a goat. The glove encasing his cock was so tight he felt as though he were being strangled, but he didn't dare remove it. Not yet.

"Good." She panted as he stretched her wider with the third knob. She bit her finger to keep from crying out.

"Do better." He couldn't recall the last time a woman had driven him to this point of desperate need. He used subs and the venue of the BDSM world to pleasure himself and ease his needs, but Caitlin had picked him up and taken him to an entirely new world, one where it was just the two of them, no pasts, no rules, and no limitations.

His rule of having sex only once with any sub had been shattered. He wanted only one woman. Caitlin. And right now, he needed her wild. For him. Only him.

Picking up the vibrator, he teased her glistening slit. She was wet and slick. He eased the pink shaft in an inch at a time and continued to coax the anal toy deeper. His breath caught in his throat as her tight rosette opened and swallowed the fourth bead.

"Oh-oh," she whimpered. "That felt really good."

Damon slid the knobby probe out nice and slow, pleased with her cries of pleasure as each bead glided out then popped back in. He continued with smooth strokes until she rocked on her knees, encouraging him, helping him. He flipped on the vibrator in her pussy.

She yelled, and her head shot up. "Oh. My. God."

"Like this, do you?" He played with the anal toy while the vibrator inside her pussy thrust and hummed and the clit tickler tickled.

"Shit—what's not—to—like?" Her voice ended on a strangled scream when he flipped the switch on the probe. She shrieked, her ass tipping higher.

He loved her response. She didn't hold back, didn't pretend. He had the feeling that, with this woman, what you saw, was what you got. Her body told him how she felt. He had to have the words.

"Tell me how you feel." He was going on desperate.

Caitlin lifted her head, revealing her long, smooth throat. "Alive—there—and my clit, it's as though it's connected to my—my ass—like the vibrations are fucking each other."

Damon continued, stretching her, teasing her. And himself. His balls were strung so tight he felt as if they were being squeezed through a very small opening and warned if he didn't find release, they just might burst. The pain in his thigh was gone, replaced by a more desperate and immediate need that came from denial.

Caitie wiggled her hips and moaned. Her beastly prince was right. There were nerves, lots of never before felt nerves there, and they were as sensitive to his touch as her nipples to a breath of cold air. She groaned when the last bead popped inside with a bit of discomfort and a slight burning sensation, but no pain.

Pleasure engulfed her each time he slid the toy out and then in, her body eager and welcoming. He flipped the vibrators on and off, bringing her to the edge, then leaving her aching and desperate. With both devices off, he teased her by sliding one or two beads out, then pushing them in.

Four in. Three out. All five in. One out. Each ball on the probe added to her pleasure. "God, I like this."

The tickle to her clit increased. The feel of the round knobs moving in and out of her anus felt strange. Weird. But absolutely heavenly. Both vibrators flared to life. The hum in her ass merged and mingled with the vibrations in her pussy. The pink toy thrust and pumped, and when he angled it, the soft material scraped across her G-spot.

But as good as both toys were, it was the tickling of her clit that had her gritting her teeth to stop the scream rushing her throat. She gasped and moaned, buried her face in the pillow as the combination of so much pleasure became more than she could handle. And without realizing how close to coming she was, every nerve shrieked, her heart pounded, and the blood in her veins ran hot and fast.

The pleasure blotted out everything else in her life, and before she could even think about coming or prepare herself for it, Damon and his clever toys sent her soaring off the peak like a juvenile eagle taking flight for the first time.

She flew into a world of bright, blinding light, a bolt of lightning tearing through the clouds and setting them ablaze with exploding white-hot sunbursts. Her body buzzed, her mind blanked until she floated back to earth. Back to her beast. She was vaguely aware of him removing the toys and washing her with a cool cloth. Fresh lube dripped onto her anus then new pressure was applied and she realized he'd switched butt plugs. This one was bigger around, the tip as big as the largest bead in the other toy.

"Relax and push back, sweet."

Caitie obeyed, and the smooth plug stretched her anus open. The ring of muscle protested, more burning than with the beaded toy and more discomfort. She groaned as it forced her to widen and stretch, but she discovered the slight pain sent pulses of electricity straight into her clit, same as when he pinched her nipples.

She liked it. She lifted her head to say so, but he smacked her ass with the flat of one hand. She squealed in surprise at the sharp sting, clenched her butt muscles, and then groaned at the feel of the plug inside her.

"Naughty sub," he whispered in her ear. "I don't recall giving you permission to come. You've earned yourself a spanking." He pushed her flat and covered her body with his.

"What?" Still breathing hard, she protested. "You didn't say I couldn't."

He nipped her shoulder. "What is rule two?"

Moaning, Caitie bit her lower lip to keep herself from arguing. Before she could say anything further, a shrill scream startled her. She lifted her head, peered through the railing, but didn't see anything. "What was that?"

"Our warning that the show is about to start. Until I tell you differently, you need to be quiet. No yelling, no screaming." His arms framed hers, his fingers threading through the backs of hers. "Watch below. The rest of the guests should be arriving."

Her brows rose when she spotted a couple leaving the thicker woods, following the narrow deer trail that led to an arched shrub. "Cinderella and her Prince Charming have arrived."

She giggled when she noticed the woman had her top tucked beneath her breasts. Her partner got onto his knees and crawled into one of the bushes with a quilt, then came out and urged Cinderella inside.

"Wow. Little tunnels. Very cool." She craned her neck, searching the darkening land below. On the far side, she spotted another couple, but she couldn't make out who they were. Her impression was of a blonde woman. Could be either Wendy or Rapunzel? They faded into the shadows hugging the trees. More couples arrived, visible only while on the short length of path from woods to the stage area. Each disappeared into the dark ring or, from her view of the stage, crawled into their dens like bears ready to hibernate. Sleep was the last thing on anyone's mind, she'd bet. Smiling, she realized the couples below were front and center to whatever was going to happen in that clearing.

"I think you're right. We've got great box seats, even if it's dark down there." She hoped there would be lights, as the lamps ringing the stage didn't reach into the center.

"Almost show time. Up you go." He pulled her up onto her knees, nudged her legs apart. His hands slid up her waist and cupped her breasts. "Let's take a quick dash to house number ten, see what sweets await us."

"You're kidding." Nine had earned her a spanking, but now there were other couples nearby. Anyone could see them. Or, good lord, hear her.

"Nope. And remember, no screaming." The hum of the vibrator against her nipple nearly made her shriek.

Another scream came from somewhere below, but Caitlin's mind was focused on the man behind her and the show where she was the star. He teased both nipples, then had her sucking in her breath as he trailed the soft, nubby silicone down her belly and zeroed in on her throbbing clit.

She jerked and was grateful for his arm banded around her. With little choice, she came hard and fast, whipped and thrown into a violent orgasm. She whimpered when he removed his finger. Spasms still rocked her insides and each time she contracted her muscles, the butt plug set off a new wave of explosions.

"That was a taste of what's coming, sweet Belle," he whispered in her ear. He jerked his hips, letting her feel his magnificent cock stroking between her parted legs.

Damon rose to his feet behind her and held out his hand to help Caitie up. He yanked off his penis glove, and her heart jumped to her throat. He was thick, the veins pulsing and twining around his cock like vines. His mushroomed head had deepened to a rich red-purple, a color in the past reserved for royalty.

And hot damn, this man was her prince.

"Oh, Sir, you look as though you need emergency attention to ease your swelling." She licked her top lip and wanted to fall on him like fleas on a dog. Her mouth watered at the thought of sliding her lips down his cock and swallowing him.

He fisted his hand around his shaft and stroked slow. "I'm afraid my poor cock wouldn't last if you did what you're thinking of doing." He slipped a foil packet out of a small pocket on his hip and handed it to her. He held her gaze. "No skin to skin. Or mouth. Condom only."

"Or?" God, it would be worth a spanking to touch him and do whatever she wanted.

"Or you might just end the fun. No candy for naughty subs."

No more candy? That was unacceptable and therefore not worth the risk. She removed the condom and positioned it right over his weeping slit. His hiss of air made her smile as she used fingers from both hands to unroll the latex over the soft head, taking her time. Her touch firmed when she started down his hard length.

He felt so damn good. She needed so much more so she fisted her hand around him, making sure not to touch him. A thrill of lust zipped deep into her center. His girth was so wide, she couldn't touch her thumb to her fingertips. Slowly, she eased the latex tube down his shaft.

Damon sucked in his breath. "Belle." His voice was low with warning.

Caitie grinned. "No skin to skin." He hadn't said she couldn't use her whole hand to apply the condom. As soon as the latex covered him from tip to hilt, she stepped back to stop herself from sliding her fingers down and over his sac.

Another shrill scream, this one much closer, had her whipping around. Gripping the rail, she searched below and spotted a woman running out of the forest. Her blouse was pulled down over one breast and her skirt rode up her ass. Good grief. What was it with exposed boobs? She shook her head. The woman shrieked, shouted that a wolf was after her.

"Oh, my god. Are there wild animals in the

woods?" Caitie leaned over the rail to call out a warning. She wished she had her rifle to scare off the animal.

Damon covered her mouth. "Shh. Not a word. No talking from this point on."

Suddenly, as though God's hand had flipped a switch, soft lights winked on. The branches and leaves in the trees surrounding the stage twinkled. Her eyes went wide with delight. There were thousands of them, some small, some larger rounded globes, enough to light up the entire clearing.

From the tallest tree at the far end, a large yellowish-white lamp glowed, a moon nestled among the stars. The woman below ran into the pool of simulated star and moonlight.

"Help! The wolf is after me! Help me! Someone help me!"

The sudden snap of a whip startled Caitie, drawing her attention to the man striding onto the stage. "Oh, good heavens," she whispered. "It's Red Riding Hood and her big, bad wolf." And damn, the guy was seriously built. She too might scream if a hunk was chasing her with his cock leading the way. She licked her lips. Scream with giddy anticipation, that is.

She watched Red kneel and submit to her Dom. "This is our show?"

"It is." Damon closed one hand over breast, his fingers playing with her nipple. The other manipulated the butt plug, twisting and turning it, pushing it in, pulling it almost out until she moaned and wiggled her hips. It was hard to focus on what was going on below when he was making her body sing. His hands trailed over her belly, leaving a path of heat and need. She sucked in her breath, waited for him to snake his finger into her pubic hair and find her clit.

But instead of a bare finger, the tiny vibrator hummed to life. She bit her lip to keep from crying out.

"Payback is a bitch, sweet. Punishments come in many forms. No noise. Not a sound."

God, if this was his idea of punishment, she'd have to make sure she did a lot of disobeying. Feeling herself ready to crest, she drew in a deep breath, then cried out when he shut off the vibrator, sending her crashing back to earth.

She moaned and understood. Pleasure and denial made for a very effective punishment. "Not fair," she grumbled the groaned when the toy on her clit came alive. Three times, she protested aloud and each time he revved her to the point of orgasm, then stopped. Caitie thought she just might go mad in a very delicious manner.

"Don't think I don't know what you are up to, little sub. Denial makes for a very effective punishment, sometimes more so than a spanking." He removed the vibrator, then the plug, and dropped them into the box.

She bit back her protest. Damn the man.

Below, bathed in light, Red and her Wolf were putting on quite a show, which got Caitie even hotter and more desperate for her candy from house number…nine? Ten? Eleven? God, she was losing count. The way Red was screaming, it was a sure bet the woman was enjoying her orgasm. Dammit, she wanted to come right along with Red Riding Hood.

How could this be such a turn on? She'd never figured herself to be a voyeur but had to admit, she was hot and bothered and her Dom, her cursed prince, kept her right at the peak, ready to topple. The show continued, and after watching Red suck her Wolf's cock, Caitie was desperate for her own release.

"God, I want you, Damon. Sir. Don't make me wait." She turned, reached out, but he caught her and forced her to face forward.

"Watch Red, my naughty sub. That is your fate tomorrow."

Red had her ass in the air, and her wolf was spanking her. Caitie cringed at each loud slap even as her gut clenched and her clit throbbed.

"Hold onto the rail, Belle."

She grabbed it as he yanked her hips back so she was bent over. She bit her lower lip. Was he going to spank her right now? Right here? She wanted to protest but sucked in a breath when his palms circled her cheeks.

Needing to feed the beast inside, Damon nudged her feet apart, his actions a little rougher than he'd been with her before. "As much as I want to turn your sweet ass as red as Little Red Riding Hood's, I can wait. For that." He slammed his cock inside her pussy, felt her moist heat seep into him, and couldn't stop the groan from escaping. She pulsed and throbbed around him, her sheath as tight as his glove. She contracted her muscles.

"Fuck." God, it felt as though she were giving him a combination hand and blowjob. "So damn good, so sweet. Squeeze me harder, faster," he ordered, needing her to push him as he pushed her.

Moaning, she thrust back, taking him deeper. Over and over, hard and soft. Dom and sub, equal in their needs, each at the mercy of the other. He swore and groaned. She moaned and gasped.

Sparing a glance at the show below, Damon gripped her hips, tipped her ass higher so he could watch his dick plunge in and out, faster, and faster.

His beauty whimpered and cried out. He pumped his hips, taking her harder. He tingled from head to toe, and the base of his spine felt as though someone had applied the hot end of a plug with exposed wires.

Down below, the wolf shouted, "Now! Now! Now!"

"Come, Belle," Damon urged. "Let's show our staring couple we enjoyed their performance." He gasped for air. "Scream, my lovely Belle. Scream for your Beast." He thrust harder, faster, deeper, his hips pounding against her ass.

His Belle bowed her back, and when the head of his cock hammered that sensitive spot over and over, she shrieked. His thrusts ignited hidden caches of desire that exploded around his cock like a string of firecrackers.

"I'm going to come," he ground out.

She gripped the rail, and he hoped it held and they didn't both shoot through with the force of his fucking.

Voices rose as one couple after another added

their joy and release to the dramatic and sensual melody rising from below. At stage center, Red screamed. As though an invisible conductor slashed his baton, high to low, scream after scream burst through the night, a resounding crescendo that reverberated through him and into her.

Damon's string of fucks joined others. He drove into her one last time. Caitlin threw her head back as he let go. Her pussy clenched around him. Her scream merged with his shout as they soared through the treetops.

Chapter Nine

Caitie couldn't remember ever having such a wild, wonderful weekend. The picnic dinner, the tree house, the show, the sex had been surreal, her own fairytale. She sighed. Even the return to the tree house had been magical. The rope bridges had been like walking on glowing-white rainbows, and above her head, the lights strung in the trees, as well as the sight of that beautiful miniature house all lit up, made her wish her dreamy weekend could be real.

How many times during her childhood had she longed for a place where she was free for just a few hours? She'd never had a place she could go to be alone. After her rough start to the event, she was very glad she'd accepted the challenge and stayed.

She sat on the back deck where she and Damon had eaten much earlier just soaking in the calm evening and thinking about the afternoon of wild and wonderful sex followed by an evening of absolutely out of this world sex. Who would have thought she'd get off watching another couple go at it and knowing others were doing the same.

Wow.

That one word summed up everything that had happened so far. A loud, haunting hooo-hoo had her searching the trees. To her delight, the owl swooped down and flew over the deck, right above Damon's head.

"I had the best time, Damon."

He sat propped against a pile of pillows beside her, a bottle of water in his hand. The man kept telling her to hydrate, hydrate. She chuckled. Sex was thirsty work.

"What's so amusing?"

She held up her own nearly empty bottle of water. "This." Then she spread her arms wide. "All of it. I feel so free."

He put his arm around her and pulled her close. "Tell me about your family. I know your mom died, that you took care of her. You must have been very young."

Caitie cradled her head in the hollow of his shoulder and neck. She smiled sadly. "Mom was diagnosed with MS when I was seven. My brother and sister were barely two—fraternal twins. By the time I was thirteen, I was running the house and taking care of the twins."

"Your father?"

"He left. Decided he didn't want kids and family and the responsibility of caring for a sick wife. He sent money, was at least responsible in that manner. He died when I was sixteen in a car accident involving a drunk driver. He'd left my mother as beneficiary to his life insurance, so that helped when she got too ill to be left alone while I was in school."

"No other relatives?"

"None willing to help." She still remembered at fourteen, hearing her mother beg her eldest sister for help and crying when it was clear there was no help coming. That was the night Caitie grew up and knew she'd willingly give up everything and take on the role of caretaker, nurse, babysitter, housekeeper, and all the other myriad of duties that landed on her shoulders.

Damon shifted to glance down at her. "You had family, and they left a young child dealing with something most adults can't handle?"

The outrage in his voice and in his face warmed her. She reached up to smooth the angry lines from his forehead. "It was what it was. And it's in the past. We survived. All of us. I have no regrets."

"So how did you go from caretaker to rancher?"

"My sister, Madison, was a horse nut. She used to hang out at the stables not far from our home. She mucked stalls and earned riding lessons. The owner rescued a couple of abandoned and abused horses and gave my sister the job of taking care of the animals. She went there every day before and after school. I helped her out when she couldn't do it because of school or illness."

She smiled softly. "The owner pretty much gave her the horses. When she was ready to go to college, I was at a crossroads, trying to decide what to do with my life. I remembered how much I'd enjoyed the horses. For those precious hours, I was at peace. I couldn't spend as much time at the stables, but the times I did spend there are among my happiest memories. So when Madison was ready to go to college and needed a place for her horses, I took my share of the life insurance and the sale of the house and bought some land with an old farmhouse and a barn that looked as though a breath of air could bring it down."

Damon rubbed a strand of her hair between his fingers. He couldn't imagine being responsible for three lives at so young an age. Certainly, he'd only thought of himself as a kid and teen. His admiration for her grew. Her need to be in charge and in control made sense, as did her deep-seated need to give it up for a time. And give it she had. She'd far surpassed his expectations. And humbled him in the process. He smiled to himself. His Belle was quickly taming her beast.

He let his gaze roam her face. Her features were soft in the gentle light from the moon, stars, and the twinkling bulbs in the tree. He could sit with her forever out here with only their owl and the sound of crickets for company. "When did you lose your mother?"

"Seven years ago." She tipped her head back. "What about you? Do you have siblings? Are your parents alive?"

He stared through the canopy of leaves at the round globe of the moon. He never talked about his life, but right now, with this woman, it seemed not only fair but right. "I have no family. I was dumped into the system when I was three and bounced from home to home." He gave a bitter laugh. "I guess you could say I've had more parents and siblings than most, yet I have none."

"That's sad, Damon."

He shrugged. "I got by." By closing himself off, using anger to hide the hurt, and later, getting into trouble by taking what he needed. "Got into trouble. Judge gave me a choice, jail or enlist. And that's enough of my sad, pathetic past."

Caitlin patted his uninjured thigh. "I said once before I'm a good listener, but you're right, past is past. So what do you do when you're not being a Dom at Pleasure Manor or building fantastic tree houses?"

Relieved that she didn't want to dig into his childhood or pry into his military service, he rubbed his chin on the top of her head. She felt good in his arms. Just holding her, enjoying the feel of her, the sound of her soft breathing, and the way her hand rested lightly on his thigh. It shocked him to find he actually wanted to simply spend time with her— non-sex-related time.

She was a woman he could be friends with. Go out to coffee and just share conversation. He grinned. Of course, the sex was more than awesome. "I do odd construction jobs. Remodels or repair work mostly. Some yard jobs like fences, decks, and patios." He pulled her close. "And yes, a few tree houses here and there. I'm mostly a one-man shop unless I need help. Then I hire a crew just for that job. Compared to saving horses, my job is just a job."

"I think you're wrong about that, Damon." Caitlin pulled away, shifted until she sat facing him. "You do good work, and I'm willing to bet those who hire you are more than happy with the results. You give them joy and pleasure." She indicated the tree house. "Maybe you give them dreams. You put yourself into your work, your love for creating. It shows."

"My love for creating?" He'd never thought of what he did as creating. His projects were jobs, a way to earn income so he wasn't out on the street. Being his own boss meant he could set his own hours, work when he needed, take time off if he was in a dark place. No, she was being fanciful. "That's painting a prettier picture than reality. I'm just a simple man."

Caitlin laughed. "You, Damon, are far from a simple man. I'd bet my ranch that you are one of the most complex men I've ever known. Like it or not, you are an artist, and this tree house is one of your masterpieces."

Her assessment was scary. No one had ever seen through the hard, cold shell to the man hidden deep in the center. He thought of that photo, of how she'd seemed to see into him, and again earlier in the day, or yesterday. Yeah, she saw far too much. But surprising, it didn't scare him or make him want to run.

Yeah, he could see her becoming a friend and wasn't sure if that was a good thing or not. He rose, his leg stiff, the muscle tightening. He bit back his oath, determined to hide his pain from this woman who saw far too much. He held out his hand. "Let's go to bed."

She blinked up at him. "You're not serious?" She wasn't sure she had the energy to go another round.

Laughing, Damon tugged her up. "To sleep, my lovely Belle. Even a beast needs to recharge."

Inside, they undressed and slid into bed.

Damon pulled her into his arms, cradled her head on his chest, and listened to her soft breathing as she fell asleep. Overhead, through the open skylight, he heard the soft calls of the owl and wished he dared slide into sleep with his sweet Belle.

****

Caitlin woke during the night in the heavenly bed beneath the open skylight. She'd fallen asleep with her very own prince, in her very own miniature castle. Overhead, the wind rustled through the trees, and the lonely call of their owl drifted into the tree house. Stars winked above. She snuggled deeper. The bed with its feather comforter and mattress top along with the Egyptian cotton sheets was like sleeping inside a cloud.

She turned and stretched out her arms, needing to feel Damon and to prove she wasn't dreaming. His side of the bed was empty.

Sitting, she frowned. A low sound from the other room caught her attention. "Damon?"

The moan came again. Caitie grabbed the robe she'd used after her shower and left bed. She found him thrashing on the couch. A slanting beam of moonlight revealed a face twisted with pain.

He called out, flung out his arm. Caitie quickly realized he was trapped in the throes of a nightmare. Unsure what to do, she went to him. She knew from the many vets on her ranch not to touch him in case he thought she was an enemy and tried to attack in defense of whatever stalked his mind.

She turned on the lights. He'd removed his leather pants and slept in his own skin. A quilt was twisted beneath him, half on the floor. She couldn't

113

stop herself from staring. Even asleep, the man had the most impressive body she'd ever seen.

She frowned when she spotted a long, deep, ragged scar on his upper thigh from just shy of groin to his knee. The muscles were taut, and spasms rippled beneath the puckered skin. Good lord. No wonder he limped. She sucked in her breath and sat on the edge of the couch. She knew enough to know he was both lucky to be alive and to have his leg.

"Damon. I'm here. Can you hear me?" As though she were gentling a frightened horse, she spoke soft and low, calling his name. At the same time, she slid her palm up his thigh, her touch faint and gentle, applying more pressure so she didn't startle him. When she was able to touch him fully, she began massaging his thigh with her thumbs, using long, smooth strokes.

Trapped in his nightmare, Damon lashed out. He heard shouting, screaming, and shrieking. He tried to stand. Couldn't. Hurt—bad. His men. They needed help. Ambushed. *Fuck.*

"Can't get them. Can't save them." The pain in his thigh took his breath away. Had he lost his leg? The pain. Breathing was labored, and his heart pounded. He was weak, everything going gray, as though his life was draining from his body.

"It's all right, Damon. You're dreaming."

The gentle voice of an angel threaded through his nightmare, soothing, calming. Heaven? He tried to open his eyes, but the light was too bright. "Not—dream. My men. Killed them."

"Wake now. You're safe. You're with me."

Safe. The soft, low voice promised he was safe.

"No!" He didn't deserve to be safe. Or soothed. His men were dead. He was not. Families destroyed. His fault. Pain had him gasping. Pain he deserved.

Except the pain was fading, replaced by warmth seeping into him. He relaxed as hands unknotted muscles and warmed him, as his angel talked and tore him from the grips of hell. He opened his eyes and blinked. An angel in white sat beside him. Not an angel. *Caitlin.*

He tried to sit, but she pressed him back against the couch.

"Stay." Her voice was gentle yet as firm as her hands when they shifted down his thigh to his calf, then up, her magical fingers finding the painful knots and untangling them gently. He closed his eyes, embarrassed and ashamed of his disfigured thigh, the weakness of his nightmares, both daily reminders of his failure. He waited for her to ask questions, but she worked in silence. His body relaxed. The back of her hand brushed the side of his dick. He stirred.

"God, Caitlin. You have to stop." He was too vulnerable after a nightmare. He needed to be alone and didn't deserve to have this woman easing the anguish of his dreams or the pain. But he wanted her. Under him, his cock buried in her pussy. He wanted to forget and lose himself in her.

For the first time since his injury, he felt alive and whole, and it was due to Caitlin with her golden eyes and earthy nature. No pretenses, no games. When most women would be horrified or repulsed, the kindness and empathy in her gaze never wavered. Empathy, not pity.

"Tell me what haunts you, Damon. I'm guessing you were in the military. What happened?"

Damon clamped his lips tight. He never talked about it, couldn't. Yet with this woman, he found he wanted to share the horrors of his past.

"I killed my team," he said bluntly.

"How?"

No shocked gasp. No horror. Just calm acceptance. "I was a SEAL. My team, along with another, was sent to carry out an extraction. The enemy found out and set a trap. My men and I went in first." His heart pounded, and he couldn't hear or even breathe.

"I'm here, Damon. Breathe. Tell me."

Her fingers kept massaging, kept him grounded, and her voice pulled him back from the shadows, from the explosion and the heat of the blasts. "Ambushed. I was hit. My men tried to get me out. Told them to leave me. They died trying to save me. The other team came in, got me out. Too late for my men." A painful sob was wrenched from his chest. He tried to hold it in, keep it from bursting free, but the gates flew open. He covered his face with his hands as tears he'd held back forced their way to the surface.

Caitlin murmured softly, her fingers working their magic as he finally let the pain out of his soul.

"Not your fault, Damon. Not your burden to carry."

He shook his head, unwilling to tell her the rest. It was his fault. But had he not done what he'd done, it would have been the other team who'd died. No matter what, he was fucked over. He shoved it from his mind and concentrated on his angel. On his beautiful Belle.

Finally, his mind relaxed even as his body tensed—with a new pain. The slid of her fingers on his flesh, brushing against his dick and balls stirred other needs.

"You need to stop, Caitlin." He didn't want to repay her kind act by turning it into self-satisfaction even though he wanted her more now than at any other time during their day together.

Caitie would have to be blind and totally self-absorbed not to see Damon's cock lengthening and thickening or feel the tenseness beneath her fingers that had nothing to do with his injury. His frantic gasps and moans became shallow struggles as need swept the last of the nightmare from his mind and the taut muscles in his thigh relaxed even as other parts stiffened.

"Much better, isn't it?" She pressed deep, pleased to see the brackets of pain around his mouth gone. She grinned when his jaw tensed. Her first impression of his being a wounded animal had been spot on. She couldn't begin to understand what Damon suffered.

He opened his eyes, and she met his gaze, saw the residue of his nightmare in his eyes giving way to hunger. No, she couldn't take away his mental anguish, but she could ease his pain and take care of other needs.

"Yes," he groaned.

"Then I see no reason to stop." She brushed her

knuckles against his growing erection and hid her smile when his cock jumped and he swore.

"Playing with fire, little sub." He let out a gasp when she trailed her pinky into his thatch of reddish-brown curls.

"Like what I'm doing?"

"Know I do. The thigh is better." He struggled to sit.

"Is it really?" She shifted to allow him up but kept her hands on his thigh.

"Yes, the worst has passed." His breathing came in low, harsh gasps as he leaned against the couch.

"I'm glad I could help." She chuckled. "I think you've got another problem." She dropped onto the floor, kneeling between his open legs. "Yep. Found a spot that appears to be in desperate need of some TLC. Maybe I should take care of it while I'm here. And willing."

She wrapped both hands around his rock-hard cock and gripped him firmly. She squeezed, released, and repeated along his impressive length, mimicking her massaging movements.

He sucked in his breath, and his fingers dug into sofa. His hips jerked. "I do not believe you have permission to touch me, my naughty sub."

"You weren't complaining a few minutes ago. *Sir.*" She leaned forward and ran the tip of her tongue over his swollen crown, dipping into his slit to lick the glistening pearly drop.

He tasted salty, yet sweet. She swirled her tongue, taking time to flick the sensitive flesh beneath his magnificently flared head, then traced the ridges where the glory of his crown joined his stiff shaft.

He let out an explosive breath of air. "Shit."

"Do you like ice cream cones?" She posed the question as her tongue circled.

"Huh?" Wrapped in a thick cocoon of pulsing need, Damon frowned. His brain had gone fuzzy, and his balls ached as though someone was sticking nails into them. He was hard, throbbing, and aching for her to finish what she'd begun.

"Ice cream cones, Sir. Do you like them?" She grinned mischievously. "I do. Nothing better than a nice, fat scoop of delicious ice cream sitting on top of a big cone just begging to be licked and nibbled."

She drew her head back. "Going to lick you like a nice, tasty double-decker. How do you eat yours?"

"How do I eat what?" God, he wanted her to stop talking. Talking meant taking her from what she was doing. Good lord, what she was doing with her mouth alone had him fighting for control.

"Do you lick your treat?" She swirled her tongue as though his cock was a scoop of melting ice cream.

"Ah! Fuck me, my sweet sub."

"Hmm, nope. Gonna eat you until you cry uncle." She tilted her head to one side. "Bet you're not a licker. You, Sir, are a biter." She closed her mouth over him, her teeth scraping the sensitive area behind the crown, then sucked him deep.

"Fuck!" He threw himself back, lifted his hips, and thrust his cock deep.

Caitie grinned and eased off. His fingers dug

into the quilt when she released him. Two could play teaser and tormentor. "I prefer to nibble and take my time so I can enjoy every single lick and drip."

She fisted him, then, nibbled from hilt to tip and caught the pearly drop. She puckered her lips like a kissing gourami, kissed and nibbled, paying special attention to the thick, throbbing vein that ran from base to tip like the spine of a feather.

His shudder pleased her, as did the way he thrust his hips, offering himself to her. She stroked his shaft, her grip firm while her tongue circled and flicked and licked.

He groaned, and to her amazement, his cock grew harder, longer, and filled her hand. "I love your cock. Sir."

Before Damon could reply, she slid her mouth over his shaft in one smooth swallow. She sucked hard, taking his breath away. Blood pumped through his veins and pounded in his head. Her hands slid up the inside of his thighs, pushing them apart. He complied, giving her complete access. When her fingers cupped his balls and squeezed, the air, trapped in his lungs, whooshed out.

Opening his eyes, needing to see her, he let out another moan. Her features were set in lines of intense concentration. She lifted her head, his cock sliding out of her deliciously warm mouth. She glanced up, her eyes hungry and dark with desire.

"Is this too much for you, Damon? Are you in pain?" Using two fingers, starting near his anus, she massaged, following the thick cable of nerves to where they ended behind his scrotum. Up and down, pressing harder, lighting a fire deep in those nerve endings that fueled his every pleasurable sensation.

"Ah! Hell, yes, but don't you dare stop. Finish what you've started." He let out another yell when she clamped her lips around him and sucked him deep. Her head bobbed up and down as she rode his cock.

It was sheer torture to watch her. Her fingers kneaded his balls. The blood pounded in his ears, and he fought not to yank her onto him and shove his cock into her pussy. She'd given so much, had taken the time to ease his pain. He'd give her this.

She rose higher on her knees and took him deeper, deeper, and then opened her throat. The tight squeeze had his hips bucking. He arched his head and back. "Fuck."

She slid her mouth up his length, her tongue flicking out to tease and torment before sucking him deep once again.

His balls ached and quivered beneath her stroking fingers. One long nail scraped the skin between scrotum and anus, then pressed rhythmically, harder and faster, as she fucked him utterly and completely.

He wanted to beg but breathing was about all he could manage. His toes curled, his hands clenched the quilt on the couch, and he felt lightheaded from lack of air. Heat engulfed him, and every nerve in his body tingled with the pins and needles. He felt as though he'd been long asleep and was just now awakening, like Snow White. But instead of a prince saving him, he had his very own princess giving him the kiss of life.

His fingers slid into her hair, wrapped the long tresses around his hand, but resisted the temptation to control her movements. He only wanted to touch her, hold her as she sent him screaming up the side of a mountain. Each breath became a gasp or grunt. Cum churned in his balls, eager to empty into his cock.

The pad of her finger slid across his anus. His hips rammed up, and her head came down in one long, hard suck. Once more, she took him deep, squeezing, squeezing, her lips as tight as her throat.

"Fuck!" His roar filled the room and drifted out the skylight to weave through the treetops. Blood pounded with the force of water streaming out of a fire hose. He went stiff, his hips spasming as cum shot from his balls into his straining cock, then exploded from him in hot spurts.

Swallowing Damon's salty essence and loving it, Caitie sucked his cock until he sagged, spent. Even as he continued to shudder, she gentled her strokes, licked him lovingly, until he sighed and pulled her up onto his lap, using gentle pressure on her head.

She smiled. "I hope that wasn't breaking any rules, Sir."

His color had returned to normal, and the deep grooves of pain had eased. She kept her weight on her knees, mindful of his injured thigh.

"I believe you broke several, my wild sub." His hands cupped her breasts, his thumbs playing back and forth across her nipples.

Desire swelled inside her, like a sponge

soaking up liquid. She met his gleaming gaze. "Guess you need to punish me."

She'd never had so many stupendous orgasms in her life, let alone in such a short time. She couldn't believe it was barely Friday. What better way to begin a new day than with another big O.

Chapter Ten

Without warning, Damon shifted and straightened until he sat. He looked like a man ready to take control. He slid her dressing gown over her arms and off. "Lie across my lap, my naughty sub."

Caitie's jaw dropped. "That's not what I had in mind for punishment, Sir. Maybe you could punish me like before." She wasn't ready to try spankings, dammit. She wanted another wild ride.

He lifted one arrogant brow. "Are you arguing with me?"

All play was gone from his face, and she realized that while he'd given himself over to her, he was back in charge. He was her Dom, not a playful lover. Chewing on her lower lip, she wrinkled her nose. "I'm not into spanking or pain, Damon."

He reached out and gripped her chin. "You're choice, Ms. Olsen, is to do as I asked or return to your bed."

Alone. The word hung there. Her body ached for his, and more, she didn't want to leave him alone with his dark dreams so she shifted until she was draped across his lap.

"Lift up."

She scooted up and felt him slide a pillow

beneath her hips, lifting her ass in the air.

"Very nice." He ran his palms across her cheeks. "Now, spread your legs." His finger slid through her crease and stopped at the entrance to her pussy. "Ah, so slick. So wet. Let's see how much you like this."

Smack.

Caitie yelped. "Hey!" She'd expected his finger in her pussy, not a slap. She rose on her arms, twisted her head, and glared at him. "That hurt." The sting from his hand seeped deep inside her and, to her surprise, sent ribbons of heat coursing through her veins. She didn't like the feeling, was not and would not be turned on by pain.

"Turn around. Down on your arms."

Obeying, she wasn't sure she could go through with being spanked and was ready to use her safeword when he landed a second stinging slap to her left cheek. Both sides of her ass burned.

Before she could protest or use her safeword, he spanked her again. She couldn't help the cry that escaped or the prick of tears. The fourth swat, something besides pain spread deep inside her and ignited a throbbing need.

"Oh-oh." She wiggled her butt, clenched her ass cheeks tight, and felt her clit come alive.

A finger eased into her pussy. "Tell me, Belle. Are you turned on?"

She shook her head. She couldn't be aroused. If she was, it was from sucking his cock, not being spanked.

"No?" He wiggled his buried finger. At the same time, his palm landed on her right cheek.

She cried out, but not from the pain. The warmth of the spanking had ignited embers of pure lust deep in her center that arrowed straight into her clit. Again, he checked her state of arousal. She heard sounds of wet sucking and wanted to bury her head in humiliation.

"Tell me you don't like being spanked."

Pain wasn't supposed to turn a person into a writhing mass of desperate need. Was it? She moaned. "This is wrong."

"Were you not told to leave behind all shame and fear? For you—for us—there is only pleasure. The method of attaining that pleasure matters not." He stroked, in and out.

Caitie whimpered. She clutched the quilt and pushed her hips back, silently begging him to continue pleasing her.

Smack!

The unexpected blow of his palm startled her. Her pussy contracted as the fresh burst of pain seared her clit. She gasped, buried her head, and tried to calm the raging need, but a trickle of cream slipped out as he tormented her both inside and out.

"You'll admit you like what I'm doing." He scissored his fingers, stretched her.

"I like your fingers inside," she whimpered.

Smack.

"Not good enough. I'll have it all, my sweet sub." He set a fast and furious pace.

Smack.

"Oh, god." She nearly screamed. "Please." How could she want this man and what he did to her? He was a stranger, what he was doing even stranger than he was. Except she felt as though she'd known him forever and lived for this moment, the pleasure of his punishment.

"Please, what?"

"More." She tilted her ass in invitation.

"More what?" He stopped and withdrew his fingers.

"No," she wailed, digging her fingers into the couch.

"Tell me what you want, sweet." He smoothed his hands across her sore ass.

The brief flare of pain stabbed deep inside her center. "You. This."

"Say it, sweet. Give me the words."

"Fine," she sobbed. "Spank me and make me come."

A tremor of satisfaction ran through Damon. He rammed his fingers deep, pleased with her scream of need and the slickness of her pussy. She coated him with her juice, and her inner muscles clamped around him, held him tight.

She quivered and shook. "Yes. Yes. Please, Sir."

He caressed one red cheek, felt her shudder as his gentle touch released a small wave of pain. It'd been so long since he'd engaged in spanking, and staring at her pink cheeks sent waves of fresh lust through his dick. Though she'd milked him dry, he was already hard and eager to fuck her.

He twisted and curled his fingers and stroked that patch of sensitive flesh. Her jerk and cry caused his balls to tighten painfully. He gasped, fearing his need might just pull his boys up clear into his throat.

He loved her firm ass, her nicely rounded cheeks glowing pinkly. His free hand parted her, giving him a clear view of his fingers dipping in and out of her pussy.

"How many times?"

"*Damon*. Sir. Please. I need to come. Just do it."

"Three more, then you'll come. Agreed?"

Caitie whimpered. "Yes."

He brought his hand down. She shrieked and rocked back. He groaned. "Count, my sweet sub."

"One." Her voice was breathless, as though she'd run for days.

Smack. He pumped hard and fast, loving how she contracted her muscles with each blow.

"Shit! Two. Good. So good. Going to come."

Damon felt her muscles tightening, felt her gathering, drawing herself in, and he smiled. "One more, sweet." He delivered the final spank, then drove her hard and fast, sending her up and over. She screamed his name, gave herself over to her orgasm.

She shook and shuddered, her pussy throbbing and convulsing around his fingers. He didn't stop, one orgasm shot into two. Then three, until, with a final scream, she went limp.

"Tell me you liked being spanked."

Small rockets still going off inside her, Caitie gasped. "Didn't. Like. Loved." Her ass stung and burned like hell, but it was worth it.

Damon pulled his fingers out. She moaned in protest.

"Let's go take care of that abused ass of yours." He urged her off his lap, then stood and held out an arm to help her up.

Her legs trembled, and she was grateful for the arm around her waist. "I don't think I will be able to sit for a while. Sir."

Her beast chuckled. "I bet I can find other positions for you. Like on your hands and knees. We have some unfinished business."

Noticing his impressive erection, Caitie groaned even as she licked her lips. "I think I can help you with your, um, unfinished business. Sir." Good heavens, talk about a kid let loose in a candy store.

She chuckled. Unlike a child who risked getting sick from eating too many sweets, she didn't think she'd have any such problem from experiencing too many orgasms. She hoped not as she still had two full days left of her weekend and like a greedy child, she planned to enjoy every minute with her Dom.

"What is so amusing?" Damon couldn't believe how wild his weekend playmate had become with each smack. Not only had she been willing to try something new, but once begun, she'd given herself permission to fully enjoy the new experience.

The remnants of his nightmares had faded, and the pain in his thigh was nothing compared to the pain in his balls and the throbbing of his cock. He wanted nothing more than to pull her to him, bend her over, and bury himself deep in her slick pussy. The need racing through his veins shocked him.

He always remained in control. Sessions with

his subs followed a plan, one he seldom deviated from. He was a good lover—considerate and gentle when it was called for, strong, demanding, and even domineering when a sub required or needed that from him. But he was seldom spontaneous.

He'd had the entire weekend mapped out with room to adjust to her needs. Those plans had been tossed aside the first moment she strode into the dungeon, anger in every line of her body and challenge sparking in her eyes. One day with this woman had him feeling alive. Human.

From a cupboard, he chose a bottle of lotion, then soaked a washcloth with warm water and glanced around. "Hmm, not much room here," he decided, leading the way back out onto the balcony where they'd eaten their dinner. He tossed seat cushions onto the wood desk. "This will do."

She wrinkled her nose as she stared at the faint light creeping through the thickly leafed branches. "For what?"

"You'll see. Wait here." Damon fished around in cupboards and drawers, picking up and discarding several toys until he found what he wanted. He grabbed a large, foam wedge and the toys wrapped in a towel. No sense in ruining the surprise.

When he returned to the deck, he dropped his bundle. Caitlin was on her knees, ass facing him.

She glanced over her shoulders. "I assume this is what you have in mind. Sir."

Lowering himself to the thick cushion, he ran his hands over her pink ass. "It's a start. I have plans for you, Belle. But first, let me take care of you." He pulled her up, positioned the wedge, and gently draped her over. He glided his hands along the slope of her spine and feathered his fingers along the crest of her ass.

Leaning back, he sucked in his breath and swallowed hard at the sight of her reddened ass and the teasing sight of her pink pussy. His pulse hammered, and his balls tightened to the point of pain. He couldn't remember the last time, before this woman, when need overcame control. "Damn. I want to fuck you right now, hard and fast, and hear you scream, sweet Belle."

Caitie wiggled her hips. "You won't get any complaints from me, Sir. You know how much I love candy."

He chuckled. "I promise to give you all the orgasms you can handle." He picked up the wet cloth. "First, let's ease some of that burning." He set the cloth onto her ass.

"Ow-ow."

He squirted lotion onto his palms, rubbed his hands together, and then glided them over her warm ass. Her moan turned to a long sigh.

Damon took his time, moving to her back, rotating between long strokes down her spine, circular motions across her shoulder, firm pressure down her arms to her elbows and back up. He followed the curve of her sides, his fingers sliding over the exposed swells of her breasts. He smiled as her breathing relaxed beneath his touch and sighs turned to kittenish purrs.

More lotion, and he moved to her thighs, using both hands on one thigh, slowly making his way to her knee, then lifting her leg, tucking her foot beneath his arm so he could stroke from knee to crotch. Setting her knee onto the cushion, he repeated his ministration on the other and leg, again setting her knee right where he wanted it so he had a prime view. He spent a few extra minutes stroking the insides of her thighs until she wigged her ass restlessly. Her breathing turned quick and shallow.

He swallowed a groan. With her knees apart, he was free to look and appreciate her sweet offerings. Moisture gathered in her slit and leaked. His need flared hotter than a forest fire. Sweat tricked down the center of his back and gathered at the base of his spine. Oh, yes, he definitely felt human again.

"Ready for me to fuck you?" He slid one finger across her soaked pussy, then up into the soft, swollen folds of her pussy lips, stopping short of her clit.

"Yes. Please, Sir. Fuck me hard and fast."

He took the time to sheath his cock, then parted her ass cheeks.

Caitie gasped when he licked her long and hard from clit to that place where no man had ever plundered. She shivered when his tongue probed, then relaxed when he shifted.

Something wet hit her anus then his finger probed. "You're not—" She broke off the words, not wanting to challenge him. New experiences, he'd promised.

"Just more play. You enjoyed what we did before, didn't you?" He eased one finger in, pushing past the tight sphincter of muscle.

She sucked in her breath. As before, nerves

flared to life, and like a ridge of connected mountains, those pulses traveled from anus to clit. She protested when he pulled out, and then groaned as he eased two fingers in. Again, there was brief pain as he stretched her, but she relaxed, breathed, and pushed back.

"You are so tight. I want to fuck you here. Would you like to try it?"

"Yes. No. Maybe." She glanced over her shoulder. "You're bigger than that plug thing.

He smiled as he wiggled his fingers. "But you like this?"

Her eyes fluttered closed as he stroked his fingers in and out. "Yes."

"Good." He removed his fingers, squirted more cool liquid on her.

Something much bigger pressed for entrance. "Sir?"

"I'll go slowly. If it's too much, use your safeword." He stilled. "Caitlin, remember I won't stop unless you say Red. Stop or no have no meaning during BDSM play as the user often doesn't mean them."

"I understand." His reminder of using a safeword if needed reassured her. She lowered her head and took a deep breath as he slathered her with lube, massaging it inside her. And then came the stretching. She tried to relax and press back. She gasped and panted. It hurt, and she wasn't sure she could handle the pain.

She didn't want to chicken out and stop the play. Her reasons for participating were to gain new experiences because sex had become boring. And to relinquish control for a while. So far, she could say with absolute certainty she had not been bored for a single moment in her time with Damon and she hadn't regretted giving him control, so she bit her lower lip and held her breath.

"Breathe, my brave Belle." He slipped a hand beneath her and ran the pad of his finger across her clit.

Caitie sucked in a sharp breath as he rubbed and caressed, all the while working the head of his cock into her opening, stopping to let her adjust, then easing a bit more. She stretched her hands out, her fingers seeking something to grip as her body began that wonderful climb up that majestic mountain peak called Nirvana.

The flare of pleasure dimmed for a brief moment when pain flared as the head of his cock pushed past that ring of protective muscle. She cried out. "Are you in?"

"Nearly there. Push back. Now."

He plunged his sheathed cock into her, filled her. Nerves only recently discovered burst into bright life, flooding her hot need. She squeezed her ass cheeks and heard his shout. She cried out at the answering burst of pleasure from her clit.

"Feels good." Damon groaned, one hand still tormenting her clit as he kissed her along her shoulders.

"Yes." She couldn't stop squeezing, couldn't stop her body from making that climb. "I need to come, Sir."

"Tell me I know what's best for you."

"Yes, Sir. You know what I want." Damn, she

wanted to come, needed him to press harder, circle faster.

"You won't come until I give permission, will you, my sexy Belle?"

And risk him stopping? Not on her life. "No, Sir."

He parted her cheeks and eased in further. Her whimpers and cries came from pleasure, not pain.

"Feels good. So good." She tightened around him, each contraction sending jolts of need from ass to clit.

"Fuck." He groaned. "I can't hold on much longer. You're so damn tight, so hot."

Each shallow breath Caitie took became a pant. She'd never known that being fucked in the ass could be so good. Yes, there'd been pain, but the pain in its own way had only ignited her pleasure. She gathered herself, ready to grab her release. Her cry of triumph slid into a wail when he removed his finger from her clit. Damn. She ached and throbbed, and she was hyper aware of his cock filling her ass.

"Don't stop. Need you," she begged.

"Got me." He took her to the edge, then again, his fingers were suddenly and shockingly gone.

"Damon, please," she cried. He shifted. Afraid he was going to pull out and stop, she opened her mouth to beg, then shuddered in ecstasy when something hard and thick eased into her pussy.

"Oh-oh." It was huge, and with his cock in her ass, she felt overfull, as though she had two cocks buried inside her.

Damon needed this woman more than he'd ever needed any other. She wasn't afraid to stand up to him or make him work for his pleasure or hers. He felt so gloriously alive. *He was alive.* The words burst out in song in his head. He was human again. It was intoxicating, and he needed more.

He flipped the switch of the dildo. The vibrations in her pussy were arrows of exquisite pain assaulting his balls. His shout joined hers. Wiggling the sex toy and sliding it in and out was sweet torture as he felt every stroke, each toe-curling slide.

"Oh. My. God!" Her voice ended in a shriek.

"Now, Belle. Now." Sweat pooled at the base of his spine. He flipped the vibrating dildo up, gritted his teeth, and found her swollen clit, already reaching high and higher, seeking that burst of freedom to send her flying.

She lifted her head, bowed her back, and tensed around him, squeezed him with enough force to having him gasping, as though someone had shoved a fist into his stomach. "Yes, Caitlin. Yes, More. More."

She convulsed and shuddered and came. But not around his cock. Damon needed to feel her response directly.

As soon as she lowered her head, he eased both cock and dildo out and removed the condom. With hands that shook, he grabbed a couple of wipes and cleaned her, then cleaned himself before rolling on a new condom.

He lifted her, shoved the wedge aside, and eased them both onto the cushions. His thigh still ached, and he knew he wouldn't be able to handle fucking her with him on top. He rolled to his back, pulling her over him, and kissed her until they were both breathing hard. "Top me, Caitlin. Ride me."

Caitlin sat up, straddling his hips, and with him guiding his cock, she lowered herself onto him with a satisfied sigh.

"So big," she moaned as she eased lower and lower until her pussy swallowed all of him, until the head of his cock butted up against the wall of her cervix.

He reached up and cupped her breasts, his fingers tweaking the hard peaks of her nipples. With hands on his shoulders, she rode him.

Eyes fixed on Caitlin, Damon felt everything close in around him, a blanket of incredible warmth, and a thick cocoon that hid the rest of the world. There was only her. Him. Them. The friction of her pussy gliding over him, his need building, swelling, so close to the surface, he knew he couldn't last.

"Again, Caitie. Let me feel you this time. God, I need to feel you come." One hand continued to torment her breast, fondling her firm mound, rubbing and squeezing while his fingers rolled, pulled, and pinched lightly. His other hand went unerringly to her clit. He moved with her, circling, stroking and demanding and thrusting to meet her.

"Now! Can't wait." He drove his hips hard, meeting her, pounding against her. Her cry was faint as the blood drummed a frantic beat in his ears. Then everything went white and silent as he went stiff. He shouted her name as cum shot down the center of his dick and into the condom.

"Damon." Her scream joined his, and once more, she stole his breath as she gripped him, pulsed around him, providing nature's vibrator for a guy.

Holding her when she collapsed over him, he blinked and stared up into the trees through eyes gone blurry with tears. He held her there, arms around her, legs banded across hers to keep her on top of him and him inside her, and watched the first rays of light pierce the canopy of leaves, extinguishing the darkness from the forest.

Just as Caitlin had done for his soul.

Chapter Eleven

Caitie took part in the afternoon spa event planned for each woman. She'd never indulged in a massage and found it heavenly, and after, in the sitting room, she and Wendy had their nails and toes painted by two tiny Asian women who chatted and exclaimed over the gowns hanging on the closet doors.

She was the owner of a horse ranch, one who got out and mucked out stalls, rode, trained horses, and even repaired fences. It never made sense to spend the money or time on getting her nails done. Once, her much younger sister had talked her into it.

She grimaced. The pain of having a fake nail torn from her finger the very next day had convinced her the effort wasn't worth it. She held out her hands and had to admit the deep red polish and squared off nail tips looked good. Maybe she would treat herself to pretty nails once in a while.

Especially if Damon wanted to see her again. She closed her eyes. She'd been right about him being a wounded animal. And though he'd lanced his wound, there was more he hadn't told her. He'd kept Friday light, more fun and exploring rather than intense, and they'd spent a lot of time just talking, getting to know each other.

Long walks with her ignoring his limp but pleased that he hadn't tried to hide it from her, and time in that beautiful garden. She bit back her chuckle. They'd made good use of one of the benches. She didn't have much opportunity to brood or think about her time. Between Wendy's chatter and the two women who bustled into the suite to take care of hair and makeup, she was forced to enjoy the moment. Caitie truly felt as though she was in wonderland. *Princessy* was her thought. She was being pampered and treated as though she belonged to royalty and was loving every minute of it.

Her younger sister had always been girlie, but not her. She'd had to be grown up, in charge, concerned with the practical, not the fussy, and had made sure her sister went to dances and proms, events Caitie had to do without. Her evenings had been devoted to her schoolwork, overseeing her siblings' homework, and spending every minute she could with her mother.

Her heart ached. Her mom had been a born romantic and would have loved the sheer magical atmosphere of this mansion, especially the tree house.

"All done," Marie announced, giving her hair a last pat. "Let's get you into your gown.

Caitie walked into the dressing room, glanced in the freestanding triple mirror, and just stared. "You are a genius, Marie."

Normally, she left her hair long and loose or gathered in a tail or wound into a bun held with a pen, pencil, or even a stick if she was desperate.

Wind on the ranch and long hair did not always mesh.

The brown strands shining with gold and red highlights were swept up. Soft curls cascaded to her shoulders. Her gaze drifted to her face. Makeup was another feminine indulgence she never had the time or inclination to take on.

Her eyes looked bigger, her brows expertly shaped, and her mouth painted red. *Fuck me red.* Modesty went out the window when her assistant held out her gown, a slinky number in midnight blue. She shrugged out of her robe and sighed as the material slid over her naked body—a waterfall of silk.

Her first thought upon seeing the gown had been shock. She'd expected yellow or gold, like Belle's ball gown in the movie. Her second surprise had been the sheer simplicity of the garment. No ruffles, no huge, full skirt favored by all fairytale princesses. Just a sleek column that hugged her curves and flared out from hip to floor. She shifted one way, then another and grinned. The fabric felt like the wind whispering against her bare flesh.

She glanced up when Wendy came out of the bedroom/dressing room. Her gown was a pale, pale green. "You are beautiful."

"And you, Belle, are a goddess, not an innocent girl about to land her prince or a new and nervous sub. I take it you've had fun?"

Caitie giggled. "Fun is too tame a word. Best Halloween ever." At Wendy's confusion over the Halloween reference, she explained candy, houses, and trick or treating.

Wendy laughed. "Orgasms likened to candy. I love that. I might want to use that for one of my books? Would you mind?"

"Not at all. You must write sexy, hot love scenes." She knew the woman was a romance writer doing research on the BDSM world.

Wendy grinned. "I have enough material for fifty books."

A gong rang, and both women hurriedly stepped into their shoes. Caitie's were silver and sparkled. "God, I hope I don't trip or twist my ankle with these heels. I'm a boot gal."

Laughing, Wendy hooked her arm through Caitie's after they each donned their masks. "You'll be fine. Let's go. Don't want to keep our Doms waiting."

They joined the rest of the women near the top of the stairs. She smiled at Rapunzel. "Having fun?"

"The best. The clock will soon chime its midnight toll, all this wonderful, fantasy world will fade, and it'll be back to life." Rapunzel glanced away. "A very boring life."

Caitie heard the sadness in her voice and noticed the shadows in the woman's eyes. Before she could comment, Hastings' voice boomed out as he called the first of the women lined up. One by one, each glamorous beauty headed down the grand staircase.

When her turn came, she drew in a deep breath. "Don't fall, Caitie girl." She wasn't used to heels or ballroom gowns. Thank goodness, hers didn't trail the floor as so many others.

Then she spotted Damon waiting below. He

wore a tux and looked stunningly handsome with a big dash of danger with his black mask. Tall, dark, and dangerous. And hers.

He held out his hand, and that was all it took. Worry and fear fled. She only had eyes for her prince. The moment their gloved fingers touched, everything around her sharpened, and she felt as though she'd come home. She wanted nothing more at that point than to dance in his arms. Earlier, she'd offered to forgo dancing, aware of his wounds, but he'd flat out refused. She vowed to keep him from overdoing.

"Beautiful, Belle. You are not a princess. You, my love, are a queen."

She grinned as they walked arm in arm to the ballroom. "Wendy called me a goddess." She spotted the woman on the dance floor, in the arms of her macho-looking Dom, who wore a tux as confidently as his Captain Hook costume.

Caitie's stomach fluttered when Damon led her into her first waltz, holding her so close, his warmth and spicy male scent wrapped around her like a cloak.

Damon stared at Caitlin and felt his heart trip. She glowed with beauty, both in and out. His Beauty. His Belle. His Caitlin. He stared down at her mask the same shade as her gown. "Even better. You are truly a goddess, Caitlin." It struck him that he didn't want the clock to chime twelve and end whatever had taken root between them.

They'd gone from strangers, to lovers, to friends, and he found he wanted more. Recalling how he'd been determined that no other Dom would initiate her into the BDSM lifestyle, he realized he didn't want any other Dom anywhere near her. The darkness in his soul raised its clenched fist. He wanted Caitlin Olsen. All of her.

Her soft voice drew his attention back to her. "Thank you. You, sir, are a very handsome prince."

Her statement left his heart aching. He was the beast in the movie, and he suspected he was on the verge of falling in love. Unlike the beast, there was no instant transformations for him. Damon was still a beast inside, a man with too many demons to ever be a gentleman and prince like his pal Bryce. His gut ached for a woman he didn't deserve, but he was determined to hide his pain and the river of despair eating away at his insides.

Red and Her Wolf whizzed past. "Those two look like professional dancers."

"I confess I only have eyes for you, sweet Belle." Giving himself over to the magic of the setting, the music, and his woman, he laughed, twirled his goddess, and held her. He ignored the twinges in this thigh and hid the pain behind his laughter and smiles. Tonight was a night to be happy and to enjoy.

He pulled her close and just breathed in her essence as they danced and swung her away from Bryce with his Cinderella. His friend looked totally besotted, and he was glad. The man's first wife had been wonderful, never minded putting Damon up when he came home on leave, and made him feel wanted. Bryce deserved to find happiness and love again.

Damon and Caitie danced, stopped to chat with

the others, grabbed refreshments, and danced some more. His wound throbbed, but he kept going until he realized every time the music turned to a faster tempo, Caitlin made an excuse to stop. She was thirsty or she needed a break or she needed some fresh air.

At the moment, they sat on the terrace, finishing a shared plate of cheese, crackers, and fruit. The cool summer breeze drifted around them, surrounding them with the scent of jasmine and moonshine. Part of him wished they could wander away, find a nice corner in the garden, and just talk and be alone, but he wouldn't selfishly deny her the magical evening of costumes and dancing. The music started again, a fast tango. Curious to see what she'd do, he stood and held out his hand. "Shall we?"

She smiled. "I'd love to. After I visit the ladies' room. Need to wash my hands."

Not surprised by her maneuver, he bowed. "I'll wait for you here." He watched her glide gracefully around the dance floor, avoiding Red and her Wolf who were tangoing up a storm.

Anger burned in his stomach like nitric acid eating through metal. He longed to be able to give Caitie the chance to shine. It infuriated him that he couldn't move with the same energetic grace of the other couple, but worse, it devastated him to know that Caitie knew it as well.

****

Caitie was surprised to find the ladies' room larger than her bedroom at the ranch. She paused in the main section, which boasted four vanities complete with mirrors and lights. Each held baskets of brushes, combs, and small towels. Bottles of lotion and perfume lined the counters.

She stared into the round mirror, saw her flushed cheeks and sparkling eyes. Had she ever had such a good time as tonight? The ball, the music, the formal attire of the guests had turned an ordinary evening into a magical, enchanted night of love.

Her eyes widened. God, she couldn't love Damon. She didn't know him. She bit her lower lip. Okay, she knew parts of him *very* well, just as he was spot on when it came to pleasing her. The rest seemed unimportant. What did it matter whether his favorite color was red, blue, or yellow, or if he liked pasta, pizza, hamburgers, or was a steak and potato man?

A maid at the far vanity smiled at her. "I'll be with you in a minute, miss." She was helping Rapunzel with her hair.

"Thanks, I'm fine." She headed down a short, mirror-lined hall into the toilet and sink area. She took the end stall. The sound of stall doors opening, followed by running water, then the chatter of two women drew her attention.

"—didn't know he was going to be here. Sure would love to be his sub."

"Thought you said he didn't take part anymore, not since his wife died."

"Doesn't. First time I've seen him."

"Lucky Cinderella. Every woman here would love to have him for an entire weekend. Bryce Langston is one of the sexiest men alive. Rich as sin too. Can you imagine living here all the time? Sure would love to snag him."

"Won't happen, Bo. He's a Dom."

The voices faded away.

Caitie grinned. Both Bryce and Glorie had interviewed her before accepting her application to join the event. Those two women were right. Bryce was handsome enough to be a fairy tale prince.

Ready to leave her stall, she heard another voice call out, "*Jaimie?*"

The crash of a stall door startled her, as did the raised voice.

"You knew! You knew he was my prince."

The two women's voices were muffled somewhat as they went into the other room. She cracked open her door, peeked out, and caught the sparkling blue of Cinderella's gown and a slash of red from Red Riding Hood's sassy and sexy dress. Cinderella, or Jaimie, was not happy.

Caitie chewed her lower lip. "Great. Now what?"

If she left the stall, she'd be revealing her presence, and if she didn't leave, she'd be guilty of eavesdropping. Sighing, she leaned against the wall. Better to think of something else and wait for them to leave. Like how the hell she'd fallen for a man she'd just met.

And there was no doubt. She was well on her way to falling in love with Damon. She wasn't the romantic sort, didn't believe in love at first sight, unlike her sister who was in and out of love and lust as though it were a revolving door.

She sighed. All she'd wanted was a weekend of

great sex. Well, she'd gotten that and more. It still shocked her to realized she liked having a masterful man—a Dom—at least in bed. No one had ever satisfied her so completely.

She wondered what Damon had planned for them after the ball. And if she'd see him again after tonight. Tomorrow, she was scheduled to leave right after breakfast. The thought that the magical weekend was nearly done brought an ache to her heart.

The sound of a door slamming told her the coast was clear. It was time to return to her beast, the ball, and whatever else awaited. She found Damon in the hall waiting for her. She held out her hand and let him lead her inside, relieved that the music was another slow, romantic melody.

"I feel like I've stepped into the most incredible dream." She sighed as she slid into his arms. "You've given me so much."

Damon swayed and rocked with her, the music requiring little more of him than to just hold her and sway. He debated telling Caitlin to stop treating him as though he might break. While he appreciated her care and concern, he was tempted to call her on it, tell her he didn't need or want her pity. But not once had he seen any sign she felt sorry for him. She was, he realized, being sensible and stopping him from doing what he could no longer do.

And that was the bee up his ass. He yearned for the illusion of being a prince, able to dance the night away with his princess. For the first time since being injured, he longed to pretend he was whole and normal. He wanted to be the beast, falling in love before his deadline so he could once again become a prince.

Love? Could what he felt be more than a deep respect, could he want more than friendship? He stumbled. Caitie's arms tightened.

"I'm fine," he lied. The punch of realization was a hard fist to his gut. He was drawn to Caitlin, was in all probability falling for his beautiful Belle, and like the Beast, he wanted the transformation back to normalcy. He desperately longed for the curse darkening his world to be lifted. She was the light chasing away the shadows, soothing the ravaged beast, calming the raging guilt tearing him apart. How could he face tomorrow without her in his life?

"Damon, I meant what I said earlier. I don't need this. I'd be just as happy to spend the evening alone, with you. And I'm not talking about sex. We could sit in that wonderful garden and just enjoy each other's company."

"I like holding you, Caitlin, and dancing with you. You are more than I bargained for, and I don't deserve you. Let me have my fantasy, for just a while longer."

"You deserve whatever makes you happy." She cupped one side of his face with her hand. "Does it have to end tomorrow? Is there a reason why we can't see each other after this weekend?"

Staring into her eyes, Damon took that long, smooth dive into a pool murky with emotions. He plunged deep, the water closing over his head, the waters dark. He was a drowning man who couldn't see the surface. He struggled with what he wanted and what was to be.

He wanted to see Caitlin Olsen again, didn't want to let her go, but what could he offer this self-assured, confident woman who was in charge of her life? She had a ranch and a passionate purpose in life. He was a contractor with a struggling business. He had a tiny studio apartment and enough demons to populate Hell to the point of overcrowding. And his purpose? To survive each day. *Shit*, sometimes survival meant taking it one long, stinking hour at a time.

Feeling his chest contracting painfully as though he were drowning, he stepped away when the music ended. In the distance, a clock chimed. *Fuck*. It was over. Time to run before he lost himself completely in this woman who offered salvation—and so much more.

Echoes of the past buzzed in his mind, growing louder until all he could hear were screams and the blast of shells. Then came the images of grief-filled women and children. His heart pounded, and he couldn't breathe. The edges of his vision darkened. There was no saving him, no peace for him. No woman who could save him, even from himself. He was a fool to get caught up in something unreal. None of this was real. It was a fairytale.

"All good things end," he said, his voice harsh.

Damon whirled around. His thigh went into a screaming spasm, and he almost went down. Unwilling to let her or anyone see him vulnerable, he did what he did best these days. He mentally ran as though the devil and his hounds were snapping at his heels.

****

Caitie's first instinct was to run after him, but she did what she had to do. She let him go.

"Most women would go after their man." Glorie joined her, her eyes troubled as she watched Damon storm from the ballroom.

"He's not my man." God, she wanted him to be hers, or at least, give them a chance to see where their friendship might lead. Caitie met the Domme's worried gaze. "I can't do it for him."

"Do what?"

"I can't give him permission to let go of the demons that haunt him. I've met many men with similar stories, men who hold onto their guilt and pain because they're afraid to live and embrace the here and now because of the horrors of their past." He might have finally lanced his wounds, but unless he kept at that wound, it would close back over and continue to fester.

"You're a wise woman, Caitlin."

Caitie felt sad as she left the ballroom. As she picked up the hem of her gown and ran down the stairs to the suite she shared with Damon, she felt like the prince in the fable, Cinderella. But in this story, she wasn't a young woman with stars in her eyes, running before the clock finished chiming. Instead, it was her prince who'd fled the ball, and it would take a lot more than a glass slipper to bring him back to her where he belonged.

Chapter Twelve

Caitie strode through the mansion early Sunday morning. She found Hastings near the front door. "I need to speak to Glorie or Bryce."

Hastings bowed his head. "Wait here."

Caitlin paced until the butler returned.

"If you'll follow me, Miss Olsen."

She followed him down a long hall to a set of double doors. He swept his white-gloved hand out, indicating she should enter.

Caitie stepped inside and found herself in a richly appointed office. Gleaming wood gave it an old world feel, but she noted the high tech equipment. Bryce Langston sat behind his desk. Glorie, the queen, sat in a chair to one side. Caitie realized she'd interrupted an intense meeting. Bryce didn't look as though he'd slept—that was probably true of most of the participants—but he didn't have the look of a happy, well-sated man.

"Yes, Ms. Olsen? Do you have a problem?" Bryce regarded her with fingers twined and steepled.

God, the man had a killer voice. She'd thought that the first time she met him, but it didn't make her insides turn to goo. Damon, on the other hand, could do that with a single, hot look.

"I'm worried about Damon. He never came

back after the ball." She moved closer, hands clasped behind her.

Glorie leaned forward. "He returned home. The event ended with the ball."

Caitie brushed that off. "Yeah, clock strikes midnight, and poof, the fairytale is over. I get that. But Damon needs help. Hell, he shouldn't even be driving. He had a bad nightmare Thursday night and refused to sleep Friday night because of his dreams." They'd spent the entire night talking about favorite books, music, politics, and movies and TV shows. But not about his past, as a boy or his time as a SEAL. She was worried about him. He'd been like an injured animal who'd run off to lick its wounds. He needed help.

"Why are you here, Caitlin?"

Boldly, Caitie seated herself. "I want to know why he blames himself for his men getting killed. He told me some but there's more."

Bryce lifted a brow. "What gives you the right to ask?"

"Love." God, there it was. She couldn't deny it to herself or to them. She'd fallen in love with Damon. She'd never believed in love at first sight, and maybe it had taken more than that first encounter, but she was hip deep.

"Are you sure it's not just lust? You've only known this man a couple days."

Caitie leaned forward, arms on the desk. "Judging from the look of you and your partner, I'd say the two of you were feeling more than lust for each other. From what I overheard between Cinderella and Red in the ladies room, she had no idea who you were. Can you truthfully tell me you don't love her? Or want the chance to see if what you feel is love?"

Glorie laid a hand on Bryce's arm. "She's got you there, pet." She stared intently at Caitlin for a few moments. "Damon needs to tell you whatever he wishes when he wishes, but you are right. He needs help, and I think you might be the one. What is your plan?"

"My horses and the men on my ranch can help him come to terms with what happened. I've seen it happen and want to give him that chance." Not to mention the fact that she loved the man and wanted the chance to prove to him that he deserved to be happy and at peace, that they deserved their shot at a happily-ever-after ending.

"You think a horse is going to save Damon from himself?" Skepticism and disbelief laced Bryce's voice.

Caitie stood and paced. "He doesn't believe he deserves to live. He thinks he should have died with his men. He needs to get out of his head and see that he has so much to offer and experience."

"In other words, you plan to give him a kick in the ass." Glorie leaned back in her chair, a glint in her eyes.

Tipping her chin, Caitie met the Domme's glance. "If need be. If that's what it takes to get him back to the land of the living, then I'll gladly kick his ass to hell and back." Never mind he was already in his own private hell.

"What do you want us to do?"

"Bring him to the ranch."

"And if he refuses?"

Caitie firmed her lips. "Intervention. I'm sure you two can figure out a way to get him out there." *To me.*

Glorie laughed low in her throat. "I'm in." She stood. "I'll bring him to you. The rest is up to you."

Caitie nodded. "Thank you." She turned to go.

Glorie's voice stopped her. "Did the weekend live up to your expectations, Caitlin?"

Laughing softly, Caitie met the Domme's amused eyes. "I think I got a lot more than I bargained for," she replied, thinking of that spanking session. "I'm in your debt. It was wonderful."

"Pull off whatever you have planned, and I'll consider us even."

Minutes later, seated in the back of a limo, Caitie pulled out her tablet and started making notes and plans. Not once did she allow herself to think that her Dom would not come to her ranch. She couldn't.

****

Damon brooded in the dim light of his studio apartment. Curtains closed, lights off, just him, the darkness, and his demons. His bedding lay in twisted tangles on the couch, testimony of his bad night. Twice he'd woken up, arms searching for Caitlin, but his night angel wasn't there to ease his pain and bring sunshine into his life.

Shoving aside a pizza box, several empty beer bottles, and a smushed bag of chips, he picked up the remote to the TV. He flipped it on and pressed play. The movie depicting a shaggy beast and a village maid flashed across the screen. He hit fast forward until he reached one of his favorite parts. "You're so messed up, buddy. Watching a kid's vid."

But he felt close to Caitlin every time he watched it. He turned up the volume when the castle objects came to life and broke into song. He closed his eyes and leaned back against the couch.

She made him feel almost human again.

For three days, Caitlin had tamed the beast inside him. She had captivated him with her humor, trusted him even when she was afraid, and earned his respect for being a strong, determined woman. It hadn't taken him long to realize the weekend of role-play was more intense and demanding than she'd been prepared for.

Yet, she'd risen to the challenge, accepted his rules, and participated with a willingness he had to admire. Even the spanking scene. She could have used her safeword and ended everything, but he'd seen the pride in her eyes, along with a bit of fear.

Yes, he admired her. And loved her. But the night of the ball had brought home the reality and painful fact that he wasn't a prince who'd won the heart of his princess. He wasn't whole and healthy with the rest of his life spread out before him, and he sure as hell didn't deserve a fairy tale ending. No, he truly was the beast, doomed to a life alone.

He scrubbed a hand over his face. Many called him a war hero. Hell, he had a medal that said so, but the only heroic action he'd committed was leaving Caitlin. He loved her over his own needs and flat out refused to become a burden. She'd taken care of her mother, raised her brother and sister. He would not be another obligation. She was better off without him.

The doorbell rang. He ignored it. The bell sang through the studio again. And again. And again.

Swearing, he got stiffly to his feet and shouted, "What the fuck do you want?"

He yanked the door open to the jarring peal. His jaw dropped and then snapped shut at the sight of Glorie Amadori standing with her red-tipped nail pressed to the button. She wore a red silk tunic and black slacks, her two favorite colors.

He glared at her. "What the hell are you doing here?"

She smiled. "My, did you wake on the wrong side of the bed." She strode in, glanced around. "Or should I say wrong side of the couch?"

"Not in the mood." As usual, her hair was pulled back in a bun of sorts. The severe style a perfect fit for her dominant personality.

"No, you'd rather brood, mope, and feel sorry for yourself." She proceeded to open his curtains.

Light spilled in, blinding Damon. He blinked, held up his hand. "Dammit, Glorie. Have your say, then get the hell out."

"And leave you to your fun and games?" She paused in front of the TV.

Embarrassed, he grabbed the remote and flipped off the DVD player. "What do you want?"

"Besides seeing you walking among the living again instead wallowing in the darkness?" She leaned against the window frame. "Sit and get off that leg."

At the command in her voice, he rolled his eyes. "Not one of your subs, Mistress."

"Then do it because you're in pain, unless you don't mind falling flat on your face in front of me."

He knew Glorie wouldn't leave until she was good and ready so he plopped down and rested his foot on the coffee table. He rubbed his thigh. "Fine. Sitting. Now what?"

"Bryce and I are worried. You left the event early."

Damon wanted her to leave. He wanted to be alone. No crime in that. His choice. "Is there a question in here?"

"You've never left an event early. So yeah, why this time?" She paced.

"None of your business," Damon said.

"Making it my business. It's time someone took you in hand so you're coming with me. I have something to show you."

With her hands on her hips, chin jutting, he half expected her to pull out a whip and snap it. Too bad she didn't do anything for him, or he might try to use sex to get the feel, scent, and image of Caitie from his mind. "Not interested."

"Tough shit. Now get your ass off that couch and take a shower. And make it fast." She lifted a brow. "Unless you want me to join you and wash your back."

Two hours later, he was still stewing. Glorie had badgered, threatened, and refused to leave until he escaped into the bathroom, locking the door. He wouldn't put anything past the sneaky, wily Domme, who could, would, and often did change her sexual preferences to suit her mood and the needs of those around them. He'd participated in one of her threesome scenes and had to admit, the woman was good, but the only woman he wanted was out of his reach.

"Where the hell are you taking me, Glorie?"

"You'll see."

As that was the fourth time he'd asked and received the same answer, he fell back into a sullen silence.

Another thirty minutes passed before she spoke. "We've been friends for a long time, Damon."

"So." He had a feeling he wouldn't like what was coming.

"So, as your friend, I'm worried about you."

"Leave it, Glorie. This isn't something you can fix." The woman was a born matchmaker. If a relationship was broken or faltering, she just had to stick her arrogant nose in and fix it. He went cold inside.

"You wouldn't?" He eyed the passing landscape as they sped down a two-lane highway in her BMW. Fields of wheat with an occasional house, farm, or ranch. Cows, sheep, and even horses were seen grazing.

Horses. Ranch.

"Fuck!" He suddenly knew where they were headed. "Turn around, Glorie. I'm not going to Caitlin's ranch.

She smiled grimly. "Too late."

She slowed and turned onto a drive. A sign hanging over an arch welcomed them to For the

Love of Horses.

"Stop."

He stared out at pastures with horses grazing. A small herd ran alongside the car as though they were the welcoming committee. "What are you doing, Glorie?"

She stopped the car. "Saving you. Or rather, bringing you here for Caitie to do that job." She chuckled. "She'd correct me and say only you can save yourself. And she's right." She put a hand on his injured thigh. The tight muscle jumped. "Give her a chance, Damon. Give yourself a chance. She wanted you to come and see her ranch. I know you care for her. You've never left an event before the end, and the state of your apartment tells me you're in pain, and not just physical."

"Doesn't matter what I feel. Reality's a bitch." God, he longed to be her man, her hero. Her prince.

Before he could order her to take him home, a loud honk had Gloria moving forward. Glancing back, he saw a truck and horse trailer following, making turning around impossible. "Fine. We'll look, and then we're gone."

She drove into the yard. An old, grizzled ranch hand hurried to her window. "Got a trailer kissin' yer ass. Don't want that beamer to get hit. Park over there." He pointed to an area where several pickups were parked.

Glorie and Damon stepped out into utter chaos. A group of men came on the run to deal with the horse trailer while others rode across the yard. There was movement everywhere he looked. The noise level was astounding—yelling, shouting, horses calling, adding their voices to the din.

"Name's Dusty," the old ranch hand shouted in order to be heard.

"Damon." He shook the man's hand, surprised to find the grip strong and firm.

"Welcome, Damon. I'm guessing you be the new one."

"New what?" He felt as though he'd stepped back in time to the wild, wild west. Men in boots, hats, and plaid shirts went about their business. Some rode, others led their mounts.

"Let's go meet your buddy."

Glancing at Glorie, the woman shrugged. He had to hurry to address Dusty. "I think you've made a mistake. I'm just here for a quick visit. Where is Caitlin?"

"Oh, she'll be here soon enough. Never misses greeting new arrivals, be they men or horses. Now move that ass. Need your help over here."

Damon followed as four horses were offloaded. He frowned. Two were in bad shape. Rib and hipbones protruding and dull, dirty coats. Three of the animals kept trying to shy away from the men. Then Caitlin arrived. She didn't glance at him, didn't acknowledge his presence. Instead, her focus was on the horses. She spoke softly and gently to each one, then gave instructions.

"Damon, could you come over here?" She held the reins of the two in bad shape.

He joined her. "Caitlin—"

"Look at them. Mistreated, abused, and abandoned. Now they'll find hope, contentment, and happiness. They'll never go hungry or be alone.

161

They'll learn to trust and love. Their lives start here. And they'll live to be old and die here."

"I'm not a horse to be saved, Caitlin. I'm not abused or mistreated or starved." He shoved aside the abandonment he'd felt as a child. He'd gotten over his childhood a long time ago but knew he'd never forgive himself for abandoning his men.

She met his gaze, her whiskey-dark eyes churning with emotion and the sheen of tears. "You abuse yourself, Damon. You mistreat *you,* and you are as starved as any of these horses. Not of food but of acceptance and forgiveness. Like each of these animals, you've lost hope. These animals were helpless to change their situations. They couldn't fight for happiness. But you can." Her gaze turned intense. "And you will."

She cupped the side of his face with one hand. "I'm not asking you to stay for me, not even asking for you to give us a chance. I want to help you heal and find your way back."

He lowered his forehead to hers. "Caitlin…"

His throat closed off, stopping him from telling her he didn't deserve what she offered. He closed his eyes. He was better off alone, but her touch, her scent, her voice arrowed deep into his being. Some long-denied part of him screamed for what she offered.

A hard nudge to his shoulder threw him off balance, and he landed on his ass. Blinking, he glared at the black horse with sad eyes staring down at him. She lowered her head and snorted, her breath fanning his face. "What the hell?"

Caitie laughed gently. "I think you've been

claimed." She reached down and helped Damon to his feet. She handed him the reins. "She's yours."

"What?" This time when the animal butted against him, he was braced and ready.

"While you're here, you are responsible for her care. You'll feed her, clean her stall, exercise her, groom her, make her feel safe, and teach her to trust and love."

"That's a tall order for a couple hours." He eyed the mare and swore he felt a connection as he stared into her large, soft, brown eyes.

Caitlin patted his shoulder. "Oh, I think you'll be here longer."

The sound of wheels crunching gravel had him whipping around. "Dammit." Glorie rolled down her window. "I packed what I could for you while you were in the shower." She wrinkled her nose. "Might need to wash most of them first." She waggled her fingers, then she and her car shot down the drive toward the highway.

Dusty joined them, holding a large duffel bag. "Yer with me, young man. Let's get the two of you settled."

Getting him and his horse settled meant taking him into the barn and teaching him to groom the horse, then feed her, and a rundown of the daily schedule and his assigned duties. He'd listened, done as ordered, and planned to tell Caitlin Olsen just what she could do with her plan to save him.

But after his chores, he'd been shown to a dormitory-style room with eight double beds spaced along two sides. Each section had a dresser, smaller table, and lamp.

"You'll sleep here. Yo, Gunny." Dusty's raspy voice rose to a holler.

A large man with skin of dark caramel ambled over. He had his shirt slung over his shoulder. The words Semper Fi were tattooed across his damp chest. "Yo back, Dusty." He eyed Damon from dark eyes.

"Got us a new guy. Ex-Navy SEAL Damon Steele meet ex-Gunnery Sergeant Javon Washington.

"SEAL, huh? Don't got us one of them around here. Welcome to CCOB."

Damon frowned. "What is CCOB?"

"Caitie's Club of Boys." Javon grinned broadly, his teeth starkly white against his dark skin.

Damon started to tell the man he was mistaken, that he was only here for the night, that tomorrow he'd hike out of here if that was his only way out, Dusty slapped him on the back. "Give this tadpole the tour. Show him the laundry room and showers. You'll find a schedule and a list of duties in the drawer beside your bed, and Gunny here will add you to the chore roster. Dinner in an hour."

Before Damon could protest to being called a tadpole, which is what a SEAL hopeful was when entering BUD/S—Basic Underwater Demolition/SEAL—training, and to being handed over to yet another stranger, Dusty was gone and Javon was striding down the middle of the room.

He turned and cocked one brow. "You coming? No shower, no food. No chores, no food. Let's go. I be starved."

Sighing, Damon followed. What the hell for, he didn't know. If Caitlin Olsen thought she could trap him out here, toss him into the barracks, and avoid him, she was mistaken. He'd have it out with her before the night was over.

The large locker-style room—minus the lockers—held a wall of sinks, showers, and toilets that resembled tiny closets with barely enough room to turn around in. The laundry room boasted four sets of washers and dryers, and finally, the dining room had one long table. By the time he'd showered, got his laundry done, was handed his weekly list of chores, and had eaten and been introduced to half a dozen other men, he was exhausted, yet restless.

Outside, dark had fallen. He stared at the house in the distance. Caitlin's house. Why the hell had she dumped him in the bunkhouse instead of having him stay with her? What the fuck? Bad enough to gang up on him with Glorie and Bryce and take away his choice, but to then dump him out here like a hired hand?

Nope. Not going to happen. He strode down the path, intending to have it out with her. As he neared the barn, he heard the high whinny of a horse. Frowning, he stopped. The mare he was in charge of was in there. He detoured inside and found her stomping and agitated in her stall. The moment she spotted him, she tossed her head and slammed against the stall door.

"What's with you? Don't like strange places?" He rubbed her nose, relieved when she calmed. She butted her head against him. "Don't blame you."

Anger burned in his gut. He didn't like feeling as if he'd been dumped and abandoned.

Leaning against the stall door, he realized he felt abandoned all over again. Not just by his friends but by the woman he'd come to care about. Maybe it had been all about the sex on her part. But why bring him here? And if she wanted to help him, why wasn't he with her?

"Going to go find out." He took two steps away and stopped when the mare let out a shrill cry. He returned to her. "Look, I can't hang out here all god-damned night."

Yet it became clear she wasn't going to allow him to leave.

Swearing, he entered her stall, piled up some straw in one corner, and slid down. "Only for a while."

The mare nuzzled his shoulder and exhaled, a deep fluttering breath as man and beast fell into exhausted slumber.

****

Caitie rode in from doing her rounds, checking on the horses out in the various pastures. The day was warmer than normal, and she was already hot and sweaty. She slowed her horse as they rode past one of the smaller, round pens. In the center, Damon, stripped to the waist, his chest gleaming a golden brown in the sun, worked with his mare on a long lead. Javon, wearing a tank, his huge arms bulging, took the lead to demonstrate longeing, a training technique, in this case for both horse and man. The horse reared and fought the line.

Damon stepped forward, grabbed the lead, and

walked toward the horse, talking softly. When she calmed, he resumed his place beside the ex-marine and, using his body to signal the mare, got her trotting in a circle around him.

Smiling, Caitie was pleased to see that horse and man had bonded and that Damon seemed to be a natural. She listened as Javon called out instructions, corrected Damon when needed, and grunted his approval.

She wanted more than anything to be the one in the ring teaching Damon how to put his horse through her paces and be the one to teach him to ride and even take him out and show him her ranch. But she kept her distance.

It had been tempting to have him stay with her in her house where she could take care of him, be there during the night when his nightmares claimed him, or help ease the pain in his thigh, but having him here wasn't about sex or fulfilling her needs or wishes. Her focus was on giving the man she loved what he needed to find himself, and he wouldn't have done that with her hovering.

She learned from Dusty he'd spent his first few nights in the stall with the mare and, in the two weeks he'd been here, had settled into the bunkhouse. Her instincts had been spot on. The other vets who'd arrived just as damaged had taken him in hand. Damon worked from sun up to sun down with no time left to wallow or feel sorry for himself.

And when he had nightmares, he found support. Or as Dusty said, the men formed their own therapy group. They gave him what she couldn't. Understanding and a comradery only another military man could feel and give. She smiled. He might not know it, but he'd taken the first step to healing.

Putting another life, even that of an animal, first, above his own problems would help him accept the past and move on. And being around others who had their own demons would make him feel less alone or broken.

When Javon called a halt, Damon led the mare out of the pen. His gaze met hers and clashed. His were filled with resentment and heat. She wanted to go to him, cup his face in her hands, kiss him, and tell him he was doing great, but she didn't dare, so she yanked on the reins and rode away.

****

Damon watched Caitlin ride off, his temper rising. Every time he tried to go to her, to have it out with her, give her a piece of his mind, someone was giving him an order or asking him a question, or he had some stupid-ass chore to do. If he neared the barn, his mare seemed to know it was him and called. And like a doomed man under a witch's spell, he went to her.

"What the hell is it with you females," he muttered. One needed him close, the other was pushing him away. He narrowed his eyes. He'd be damned if she kept ignoring him and treating him like the rest of the men who were proud to be *Caitie's Boys*.

Fuck. He wasn't a boy thrilled to be in some secret boys-only club. Only clubs he belonged to were ones where he was a Dom and in charge. It was about time *Caitie* remembered he was a Dom. Her Dom, dammit. He should march into her office tonight and order her to bend over her desk. His dick stirred at the thought of taking her from behind, seeing her wet, pink pussy begging for his cock.

Fuck. Now he was hard as a rock. He'd been on edge since arriving, his body taut with need for Caitlin. That need grew more urgent with each passing day until he thought he might just snap like the string of a violin. Only by falling into an exhausted sleep was he able to keep his needs under tight control. A nudge to his shoulder reminded him he needed to groom Bella.

He did a mental eye roll. His horse, his name choice, Dusty had informed him. He'd had no idea what to call the horse. He'd never had a pet of his own. So he chose Belle, or Bella.

"Stupid sap," he muttered, leading the way to the barn. The motions of grooming soothed and calmed him. If he were honest with himself, he'd admit he hadn't felt as at peace with himself or the world as he did while working with his mare.

His. No one had ever given him a pet, and he didn't think of Bella as a pet but as a friend. Two needy creatures shoved together. And it was time he had a few words with another woman he'd viewed as a friend. And more.

So when the sun lowered in the sky and all his chores were done, he slipped out of the bunkhouse and headed toward the house, and yes, detoured into the barn and grabbed a carrot from the bin in the fridge and gave Bella her treat. "Now, behave for a while. I've got another woman to see."

Reaching the door to her house, he entered through the kitchen. He knew from watching her she spent her evenings in her office, often working long into the night. Yet, she was up before the crack of dawn. He recalled the tired droop to her shoulders earlier and the dark circles beneath her eyes.

He shook his head. She ran this ranch with the skill and training of a commanding officer. There wasn't a single aspect of the ranch she didn't know or handle. Dusty was her second in command, but she was very much in charge. Her need to take on a submissive role during sex made so much sense, as did her natural inclination to fight that need. It was time to remind her of that little fact.

Reaching her office, he leaned against the door jam. "We need to talk, Caitlin." He kept his tone cool and formal, even though in his mind, she'd become Caitie.

She glanced up from her ledger. "Damon. What are you doing here?"

"Having a long-overdue conversation." He noted she looked even more tired than earlier, as though she hadn't been sleeping well or had been putting in too many hours. Both, he'd guess.

"Um, you shouldn't be here. You know the rules."

"Yeah, the Caitie Club rules. But I'm not part of that club. You may have finagled a way to get me here, and I'll admit, maybe it wasn't a bad idea, but I'm not one of your hired hands. Am I, Caitlin?"

She leaned back in her chair. "No, Damon,

you're not," she said softly.

"Then why are you avoiding me. Why am I over there, with the Caitie Club guys, and not here with you, sharing your bed?"

She stood, went to her window, and glanced out. "You need time to heal."

"Bullshit." He crossed the room and turned her around to face him. "You don't think I can heal around you? That's it better for me to be there instead of here? Are you sure it's not because you're tired of me? Or maybe you really didn't like what we did during that three-day weekend."

Caitie lifted one brow. "You know very well I loved everything we did. For your information, you are the one who walked out on me. You left the ball and didn't come back. You never even said good-bye, Damon. What was I supposed to think?"

The stark truth hit him hard. It was true. He'd left without a backward glance. How could he explain he'd been thinking of her? He paced away from her, then back.

"You're right." He felt ashamed and a bit helpless. How could he fix this? And fix it he would. He needed this woman and everything she had to offer.

"Why, Damon?" She leaned against the windowsill.

"Because I couldn't tango with you."

She blinked.

He held up his hand. "Because you made me realize I wanted what I couldn't have, couldn't give you what you deserve. I can barely take care of myself, let alone be responsible for someone like you."

He strode back and forth, barely aware of his limp, which was always worse at night, at least until Dusty got his hands on it with that god-awful smelling horse crap. But he had to admit, the scar lesions were breaking up, and the pain had already lessened.

"I vowed never to put myself in the position where someone else's happiness or life could be screwed up by my actions or lack of actions." And that meant living in a vacuum. His short time at the ranch, talking with others who had eerily the same issues, had taught him he was simply sinking deeper into his own dark pit.

"And now?

Seeing the pain in her eyes, and yes, the longing, he wanted to pull her into his arms and kiss her, be her Dom, and take some of the responsibilities from her. But he was afraid of her rejection. Him, a Navy SEAL known for his cool detachment under fire. "I'm dealing. For the first time since I was injured, I'm dealing with it."

He stepped closer to her, reached out, and cupped her face in his hands. "I was so angry, so damn resentful, and even felt betrayed." *Abandoned.*

"You could have left. Had you really not wanted to stay, Dusty or one of the men would have taken you home." Her eyes searched his.

"Or I could have hiked to the road and found my way back." He grimaced. "Planned on doing just that."

"Why didn't you?"

"Because I wanted you. Wanted to become the man you needed me to be. So I stayed, told myself you were full of crap and I'd prove it to you, but, instead, I'm ready to admit you were right."

She smiled and tears tracked down the side of her face. "That's a start."

He swiped the tears away. He could actually smile and feel the knots and tension easing from his shoulders. "Does this mean we can spend some time together?"

"I think we can arrange to go riding together."

"Just riding?" He pulled her closer."

"Hmm, what did you have in mind?"

God, his mind was suddenly in overdrive. He could take her on her desk, on the floor, have her kneel and take his cock in her mouth. His blood pooled between his legs and set off fresh waves of need. Three weeks felt like three months.

"Know any good Doms?" Her voice was low and throaty.

He lifted a brow. If that wasn't an invitation, he didn't know his women. His subs. On the verge of stepping back and taking control, he hesitated. She was willing to take him now, start building that relationship. But as much as he wanted to claim her and fuck her until they were both yelling and screaming, he wanted something more. He wanted her friendship and her respect.

He bent his head, kissed her long and hard, drew her taste and scent deep into his soul. His body and mind were relieved at her passionate response, and his dick grew hard and ready for what was to come.

Instead, he lifted his head, smoothed his thumbs over her cheekbones, then stepped back, dropping his hands.

"I know just the Dom for you. He knows what you need, and he wants to give it to you. But when he comes to you, he wants to be a whole man. He wants to be your Dom and your man. The man got lost, forgot how to live, but he's coming back. Can you give him time, give him a chance? Maybe let the man and woman catch up to the Dom and sub?"

Caitlin laughed low in her throat and eased close. She stood on her toes and kissed him gently on the lips, then stepped back. "The woman would love to get to know the man."

Damon returned to the bunkhouse. For the first time since being injured, he had a reason to heal and live.

****

Caitlin leaned on the rail and watched as Dusty and Damon put a gelding through his paces. Like the mare, Damon had bonded with this animal as well, and so far, he was the only one who the horse would allow on his back. She sighed with contentment and studied the man she loved. Her plan had been a success. He'd been here just over three months, and the transformation was miraculous.

She missed him, yearned to have him with her every day and night. The occasional meal and their rides were good. Better than good. She enjoyed exploring his mind, his intellect during what she thought of as their date time. They discussed horses, the ranch, his childhood and hers, and he even shared some of his stories as a SEAL, at least the non-classified ones. But neither made the move to a more intimate relationship. If and when, it would be up to him.

When he felt he was a whole man.

An hour later, Damon trotted over.

"He's ready to take out." He yanked his hat off and blotted the sweat from his face.

"You sure he's reliable. I'd hate for you to get thrown." She grinned. "Again."

He laughed. "We're pals. He won't even think about bucking me, will you, pal?" He stroked the chestnut.

"All right. Where to?" She treasured their jaunts and outings together.

"How about our little oasis? It's not far." His glance slid from her face down her body, then back up to her mouth.

She felt that delicious shiver trip down her spine. The stand of pines near a small, natural spring was one of her favorite places, and the center of many fantasies between her and this man. The sexual tension growing between them was like a snarling K-9 nipping at the heels of a perp. Need and pure lust hummed through her, but she kept it tightly reined. *When he's ready.* She just hoped he didn't take too long.

"It's close enough to walk." The stand of trees started at her house and ended at the spring.

"Yeah, but I'm lazy. Let the horses carry the picnic stuff."

Caitie laughed. "Fine. I'll meet you in ten."

"No need. Had Josh saddle your mare."

"Pretty sure of yourself, Damon Steele."

He waggled his brows. "Nope. Pretty sure you wouldn't say no, Caitlin Olsen."

Shaking her head, she opened the gate to the large corral, large enough to hold riding lessons or work more than one animal at a time, let him and the horse through, then latched it. He rode off toward the barn, leaving her to follow.

****

Damon was nervous as teen on his first date. "Got everything, Javon?"

He slid down, pleased when his thigh didn't protest. Dusty's nightly tortures with that smelly horse ligament and rough but firm massages had done more than all the PT he'd tried. Better than going back under a knife to remove scar tissue adhered to bone as his last doctor had suggested.

"Yo. And here's your pack."

Working quickly, Damon attached a quilt, basket, and the small bag he'd dropped off earlier that morning to his saddle. He put up with the good-natured teasing from those in the Caitie Club. Everyone knew he was more than just one of Caitie's Boys, and it amazed him that no one minded. When Caitie, as he now thought of her, arrived, all teasing and crude remarks were zipped. There wasn't a man on the ranch who didn't love this woman in some fashion.

He grabbed the reins of her mare and handed them to her, then helped her into the saddle. Again, with an ease that never failed to astound him, he mounted, and together, they headed toward the back of the sprawling ranch house, then followed the trail that ran down the center of the groove of pines. They discussed the condition of the horses, the repair schedule, and Damon's recommendations for more repairs. As a contractor, he'd found himself quickly put in charge of the buildings.

"Got a crew starting next week on raising a new barn. It's bigger, with more storage."

"That's great news. The one on the property when I bought it is about to fall down."

"It's gone now. Had the men take it down. Saved what we could to reuse." He liked the idea of incorporating old and new. Old history and new tomorrows. He eyed Caitie. Was he old history or did they have new tomorrows? He'd soon find out.

When they reached a small clearing surrounded by Douglas Firs and Ponderosa pines, she dismounted. He followed suit and handed her the quilt and basket. "Talked Martha into frying up some of her fried chicken."

Caitie spread the blanket. "You didn't have to talk her into anything. All you did was grin and say please. I swear she'd walk over fire for you." It was nice to be away from the noise and what she often thought of as organized chaos and heavenly to be alone with Damon.

Damon's hands came down on her shoulders, and he pulled her against him. This woman had given so much. Because of her, he felt alive. And at home. "And you, Caitie? Would you walk on fire for me?" He turned her and stared down into her eyes

She cupped his face. "You know I would."

"I was so angry for the first few weeks I was

here."

She smiled. "I know."

He leaned his head against hers and wrapped his arms around her. "You were right. You have an amazing gift, Caitie. You saved me."

"No, you saved yourself. I just gave you the tools." Two tears fell.

He wiped the moisture and held her chin. "I was too damaged to find help."

"And now?" Her gaze searched his.

"On the mend. Still have a ways to go, but for the first time since I came home, I've found peace."

Tears ran in a steady stream. "You've forgiven yourself."

"Yeah. Dusty and the others have beat it into me that I wasn't to blame, that war is fucked, and good men die. Bad shit happens. I did my duty, have no guilt there anymore. The enemy who ambushed us is to blame. Not me."

Caitlin threw her arms around him. "I'm so glad, Damon."

"There's something I've never told anyone, not my commanding officers, not even the men here. I want to tell you." Needed to come clean with her.

"Okay. I'm a good—"

"Listener." He chucked, pulled her around so he could see her, so she could see him. "That last mission didn't go quite as planned. We had three teams, plus troops and support staff. Command wanted to hold my team in reserve, as back up. I convinced them, instead, to let me take point." He drew in a deep breath. "Had I not wanted to get in and be in the center of the action, my team would be alive. All because I countered command.

Caitie rose onto her knees. "And this is why you blamed yourself. Not just because they died, but because they didn't have to die."

"Yes." He pulled her back into his arms as the last of the weight fell from his shoulders. He held the woman he loved, breathed in her scent, and allowed himself to feel, to hope and to dream. "I still have issues and nightmares, will always deal with them, and probably some pain as well, but I hope the regrets I hold will eventually fade. Though I never want to forget those men or their families. They shouldn't be forgotten, and I'll remember the good times. But I no longer blame myself. Had it not been me and my team, it would have been another. The mission was doomed from the beginning. I could never wish that pain of loss on anyone else."

He drew back. "If you'll have me, I want to stay with you. Be part of your life. With you, I'm alive. And I feel like I've come home."

"Oh, Damon." She hugged him tight. She'd known there was more and was honored he'd shared it with her. No wonder he'd been so tormented and lost.

Holding her close, he nuzzled her hair. "I love you. Can you accept me as both your beast and your forever prince?"

Caitie tipped her head back and stared at him. "Only if you'll also be my Dom and my man and move into my house with me. I love you, Damon."

He feathered his lips across hers. "This Dom doesn't care who's in charge at the moment. He just wants to kiss you and make love to you right now, right here. In our bedroom."

"Bedroom?"

Grinning, he picked up his pack and removed a roll of paper. He pulled her down and spread the large sheet. "I figure our bedroom is about here. But up a good thirty feet."

Caitie's jaw dropped as she stared at the plans for an elaborate tree house. "Our very own tree house?" Her gaze tracked platforms, rope bridges, and a multilevel house. The entire project took up a good portion of the stand of pines, and the color printout showed that it blended perfectly, looked as though it had been planted with the trees and grown naturally with them.

"Yep. Notice the bridge that leads to the tree right outside your bedroom window. Going to add a balcony so we can sneak out and go to our own special place."

She was impressed. And amazed. "You can really build this?"

"Had the trees checked out by an arborist. A couple are too weak and diseased and will have to come down, and we'll have to do some trimming of deadwood, but otherwise, that's a very healthy stand of pines, Ms. Olsen." He rolled up the plans.

"You know I have a business. On hold for the time being, but I want to specialize in designing and building tree houses if you don't mind me taking on outside jobs here and there." He shrugged. "Even had a couple of local ranch owners ask for quotes and advice. But if you don't want me to continue with my business and want me to just work here,

I'm good with that. You have a great place here, Caitie. I'm grateful to you, Glorie, and Bryce."

"Damon, I love the idea of you doing tree houses and whatever contract work you choose. I think it's healthy for you to have your own interests and business. We'll work it out. Now, Sir. I believe you're talking far too much and not doing enough kissing." She stood, kicked off her boots, and quickly undressed, then lay back.

Grinning, Damon followed suit and glided his naked body over hers. He pulled her arms over her head. "Guess I'd best take care of my duties. Want to go trick or treating?"

"Only if there's lots of candy." She let out a long, satisfied moan when his fingers slid through the curls of her mound and settled on her clit.

"How much candy can you handle, Ms. Olsen?

"Got an incurable sweet tooth, Mr. Steele."

She sighed when Damon's mouth closed over hers and hoped the first house he took her to was a duplex. Or even better, a triplex.

About the Author

Sydney St. Claire is the pseudonym of Susan Edwards, author of Historical Native American/Western/Paranormal romances and of the popular White Series. During her career, she has been nominated for the Romantic Times Career Achievement Award for Western Historical and Reviewer's Choice Best Book Award.

Sydney takes her readers into the world of erotic romance where her characters come together in explosive passion as they solve life's problems and find true love along with the best sex our hero and heroine have ever experienced.

She credits her mother for her writing success. Encouraged to read, Susan always preferred happy endings, which meant romances were her favorite genre.

Susan resides in California. Her office is quite crowded with two small dogs at her feet, another huge girl in her recliner, and five cats to keep her company while she writes. Life gets fun when all five insist on supervising…

When not writing, she enjoys crafts including quilting, sewing, cross-stitch, and knitting. She and her husband of thirty-plus years are avid gardeners. Camping, fishing, biking, and hiking are other outdoor pursuits she enjoys. She is, of course, an avid reader and hates cooking and housework.

Contact Susan/Sydney at:
Facebook
https://www.facebook.com/sydneystclaire
Twitter
https://twitter.com/Sydneystclaire
Email
sydneystclaire@aol.com or
susan@susanedwards.com
Blog
http://sydneystclaire.com/blog
Goodreads
http://www.goodreads.com/author/show/5051440.S
usan_Edwards
http://sydneystclaire.com
http://susanedwards.com

To chat with Sydney and other Wild Rose Press
authors of erotic romance, join us at
www.groups.yahoo.com/group/thewilderroses.

Also Available

Snow & Her Huntsman
By Sydney St. Claire

Once Upon A Dom
Book Three

http://amzn.com/B00ROH9LGQ

Rylee Kincaid's business is about to go under. Lucky for her, she's found an investor. Ready to sign papers, she learns her knight in shining armor is Hunter Finnegan, the man who once gave her multiple orgasms then crushed her young, tender heart. Her world comes crashing down as it becomes clear the rich businessman intends a hostile takeover and to cast her out. Then he agrees to discuss a new deal, but only if Rylee will play Snow to his Huntsman at a BDSM fairy tale event.

Hunter has never forgotten the weekend of kinky sex he shared with Rylee in college. Unfortunately, he had to let her go to keep peace in his family. Now he's back to claim the only woman he's ever loved. He'll stop at nothing to make the black-haired, fair-skinned beauty hear the truth of what happened so long ago, even if he has to tie her up. And that's exactly what he does. But as the Huntsman reawakens the submissive in Snow, Hunter isn't so sure he can do the same to Rylee's heart.

Chapter One

Rylee Kincaid floated in a sea of joyous emotion. She'd managed to save her small interior decorating business, Interior Dreams. A short while ago, she'd been jumping with excitement. And why shouldn't she? She'd found an investor willing to inject her company with desperately needed cash, and today, they were signing papers.

Dressed in a blood-red power suit with killer heels, she led Glorie Amadori to the conference room. Rylee wore her serious, business demeanor like most women wore their accessories, even though she wanted to dance and hug the woman behind her. But her salvation was a fierce and scary woman who never smiled or laughed.

Rylee wrinkled her nose as she passed Henry, one of her brilliant and very talented graphic artists. She swallowed her chuckle. Henry had dubbed their savior, the dark haired, dark-eyed Italian woman as "The Dragon." He swore the woman scared the crap out of him.

Glorie, during her visits to check the company books, had talked with employees and toured the offices. There'd been no warmth or friendliness. She was a hard and, yeah, cold businesswoman. But did Rylee care? Nope. Someone was willing to invest and save her business, along with the jobs of her employees, and that was all that mattered.

She poured two cups of fresh coffee. Glorie took hers black and strong while Rylee liked hers sweet and light. Joining the woman at the table, she smoothed her skirt and sat, then picked up the contract to give it a final read-through. They'd agreed on terms and conditions, and later this afternoon, Rylee would take the papers to her lawyer. She barely managed to contain her happiness as she skimmed over much of the legal mumbo-jumbo until she reached the details that would put the funds in her bank account.

The company investing in her business read as *F.A. Investments Group*, and underneath—*CEO Hunter Finnegan*?

Her bright, happy mood popped like a balloon that had flown too high into the atmosphere. "Hunter Finnegan? He owns F.A.?"

Her heart jumped as the image of a tall, impossibly handsome man flooded her mind— golden brown hair, tawny eyes, and skin kissed by the sun, along with full, sensuous lips made for kissing. Once upon a time, he'd been the man of her dreams.

"Yes." Glorie sorted a pile of papers across from her.

Rylee frowned. When Glorie first approached her with the idea of F.A. Investment's interest in her company, she'd been happy and relieved. Bottom line for her had been how much they were willing to invest and what they wanted in return. The terms were tough, but fair. They'd hammered out the details, and today, she'd been prepared to celebrate.

But learning Hunter was behind the offer dimmed her optimistic outlook. Why was he interested in her business? Her gaze tracked over the contract details.

Sale of business...new CEO...owner will step down...

Reality stepped in with a one-two. Flaming arrows thudded into her stomach. The burning in her gut slid upward and flared painfully in her throat. Her eyes blurred as she stared at the contract, the words swimming before her shocked gaze.

Sell? What the hell? She wasn't selling what she and her husband Jerry had started ten years ago. She'd poured her heart and soul into her business, and if she sold it, her employees, who were her only family, would be at the mercy of strangers. No way was she giving up control. Sweat trickled down her spine while anxiety chilled her skin.

She gripped her hands beneath the table. "Ms. Amadori, this is unacceptable. Selling the company wasn't part of our deal. These are *not* the terms you and I discussed and agreed upon."

Glorie didn't bother to glance up from the papers she sorted. "Those are the terms available to you, Ms. Kincaid. Your company, as it stands, will not survive, even with a healthy dose of cash. Mr. Finnegan decided the best way to save your business is to buy it outright to gain control. This will allow him to do whatever is necessary to protect his investment." Glorie lifted her head, her dark eyes shards of obsidian. "We will have to make major changes to turn things around. First on the list, we'll have to appoint a new CEO."

"What about me?" Oh god, what about her

people? They needed her as much as she needed them. Her business was her life, especially since losing Jerry.

"You will remain on as an adviser for three months."

"And after?" Her mouth felt so dry it was difficult to speak, but she was afraid she'd choke if she tried to swallow. The acid in her stomach churned, and her heart pounded behind her ribs. Tremors of fear settled deep in her core.

"Your role here will be fulfilled. Mr. Finnegan is willing to pay you a fair price for the business, and he's agreed to include a generous bonus—if you remain to oversee the change of ownership."

Then you're gone.

Rylee stood, strode across the room, and stared out the window as she struggled to keep her tears at bay. This was a crushing blow, but she'd be damned if she showed any weakness to the woman who'd suddenly morphed into an evil, fire-breathing dragon ready to devour its prey. She loved her company, loved each and every employee. She and her husband had cultivated a family atmosphere, and she prided herself in taking care of those who'd given so much to her, especially during Jerry's fight with cancer.

People who worked for her stayed. Most of her current employees had started with her ten years ago. She could count on their loyalty, but loyalty and a sense of family didn't pay the bills. The downswing in the economy had hit her business hard, and even though the economy was improving and small jobs were trickling in, her business wasn't going to recover without a fast influx of cash.

She spun around. "This is my business. These people are my responsibility. All I need is someone to invest in my company. Not buy it. We have a huge contract in the works that will put us back on our feet. It's a done deal. I just need a bit of help in the meantime."

Glorie arched one thin, shapely brow. "Done deals are not money in the bank, Ms. Kincaid. It will take a good six months before you see any significant revenue. Hunter is willing to step in and save your business, now. Once the papers are signed, the company becomes part of F.A. Investments. Your employees, along with everything else, will belong to Mr. Finnegan."

Rylee had never hated anyone, but at that moment, she was close to hating Glorie. The woman had gotten her hopes up, and in the blink of an eye, she'd dashed them. No, the cold-hearted bitch had ground them beneath her wickedly stylish heels. Could she swallow her pride, take the hit to her heart if it meant saving jobs? "If I agree to this, what about my employees?"

Glorie removed her glasses and tucked them into black leather case. She snapped it closed. "There will be changes. We'll be bringing in some of our own people, and during the process, some of the deadwood will be trimmed. That is business, Ms. Kincaid. Interior Dreams needs fresh blood. Now, the contracts are ready. As soon as you sign each set, we'll get started."

The woman's gaze remained expressionless. Rylee's fingers itched with the urge to take those neatly stacked papers and toss them around the room. Even more satisfying, to bodily throw the cold-hearted bitch out and tell her to stay the hell away, but without an investor, Interior Dreams would be forced to close. Soon. This had been her last hope.

"Ms. Kincaid, I understand this is difficult. You didn't read the page with the amount Mr. Finnegan is willing to pay. I have to say, his offer is more than fair. You won't get better from anywhere else." She named a price.

Rylee's jaw dropped. "Nine hundred ninety-nine thousand?" She swallowed hard. One buck short of a million? Never in a million—ha ha—years would she find anyone else willing to pay that much for her mid-sized company. She swallowed hard. *But that's not the point.* Her people were more important than money.

Ignoring the hollow sickness in her stomach, she met Glorie's amused gaze. "Price isn't the problem here. I won't sign this. I want the original six-hundred-fifty thousand and the terms you and I agreed upon. Not this bait and switch crap." Holy cow, she was turning down an offer almost double the original.

Glorie stood. "These are the only terms on the table. You can have your lawyer check the contract, but it's simple enough. I'll be in contact. If you have any questions or concerns, you're free to take them up with Mr. Finnegan." She gathered her briefcase and, without another word or glance, opened the conference room door and strode out.

Rylee dropped into one of the chairs and stared

at the contract. "What am I going to do?"

In the three months she'd been searching for someone to invest in her business, F.A. Investments Group had been the only one to show interest, and now, to learn that Hunter was behind this made her furious.

Hunter Finnegan was a ghost from her past and, presently, a sharp thorn in her side. Was he doing this because she'd refused to go out with him? They'd met in college at a wild party. He'd been the campus rich kid, and she'd been there on a hard-won scholarship. Somehow, the two of them had ended up in her studio apartment. She didn't remember how they got there, but there was no forgetting that wondrous weekend of sex.

They'd talked, made love, crawled out of bed to eat, made love in the kitchen, shared her tiny shower, and yeah, more sex. Hunter had claimed her heart, mind, and body for three nights and two days. He'd left early Monday morning to go to his classes with the promise of returning that evening.

Rylee kicked a chair as she recalled how foolish she'd been. She'd waited for him, night after night, but he never came back. Didn't even call. She'd finally tracked him down on campus. "Big mistake."

Her dream man had poofed, leaving behind a slimy snake. He'd made it clear their weekend of passion meant nothing to him. He'd betrayed her trust. She'd been a foolish, naive girl playing with fire. Well, she'd gotten burned and learned her lesson. Forget the rich guys. Stick to sweet boys like Jerry. She and Jerry had been in a study group together and gone out for coffee a few times. He hadn't set her blood on fire like Hunter, but he was nice.

Glaring at the stacks of papers, hating those precise edges, she smacked each taunting pile. "Hunter Finnegan, you can go straight to hell!"

She'd seen the man once in ten years. Six months ago, he'd had the nerve to show up and ask her to have coffee with him. Said he was sorry for her loss and wanted to talk to her. Her first impression of him had left her in in awe. The college boy had morphed into a man to be reckoned with. His body was harder, shoulders wider, and in his expensive suit, he commanded attention from everyone around him. His handsome face was edged with a toughness that only made his sex appeal stronger.

A bark of laughter escaped. One glance into his eyes, and all the desire she'd once felt returned, slamming into her with the force of a rogue wave on the beach. But she wasn't going to let him drag her out to sea again. She'd told him where he could take that charming grin, hunky body, and those very kissable lips. He'd trounced on her heart once, and she'd be damned if she gave him the opportunity to break it again. He'd left, and she hadn't heard from him again.

Until today.

She was that cliché nerd on the beach who got sand kicked into his face by the bully, and Hunter Finnegan was that bully. He played fast and loose, doing whatever it took to get what he wanted, and then went on his merry way without a thought to anyone else.

Like romancing a young girl's tender heart or playing upon a grown woman's desperate need to save her business.

There was no doubt in Rylee's mind that he'd roped her in with Glorie's original offer and was now getting even with her for dismissing him by trying to take her business.

"Bloodsucking vermin. That was Hunter. Enough of this," she muttered. "That bastard's not doing this to me. He's not taking away my choices." If she signed the contract, that was exactly what he was doing, because it wasn't her decision. It was manipulation, and she'd had enough of others controlling her life.

She left home to get away from domineering parents and married a man who was a master of manipulation. She was not going to be tricked or forced into giving up her company. She snatched up the contracts, shoved them into her briefcase, and stormed from the conference room, her mood dark and angry as she left the building and emerged into the noise and traffic of San Francisco.

****

Seated behind his massive desk, Hunter Finnegan studied his business partner. "She take the bait?"

Glorie Amadori sent him a quelling glare. "The woman looked as though I'd kicked her in the teeth." The look she shot him would have turned any other mere mortal into a pillar of stone.

He lifted a brow. "You don't approve? What happened to the shark?"

"This wasn't a normal takeover, and you know it. I did this as a favor." She stood and stared down her perfectly straight nose at him. "You owe me, Hunter."

He sighed and spun the pen he held around his fingers. "Yeah, I do. Think she'll come?"

She laughed low in her throat. "Rylee Kincaid is going to charge in here, and frankly, you deserve whatever hell she gives you." She grinned. "I should go into acting. Played a most convincing bitch."

Hunter rolled his eyes and tossed the pen back onto his desk. "Got news for you, Glorie. It comes naturally, and you don't need your whips or your Domme leathers." She was a scary woman, *especially* when she was in Domme mode.

"You'd best hope I don't turn it on you. You might be my friend and partner, but this…" Shaking her head, she gathered her briefcase and purse. "Not like you to take a woman's rejection to heart, Hunter. What's so special about Rylee Kincaid?"

He stood and wandered to the corner window. Fog obscured the Golden Gate Bridge in the distance. "It's complicated." He remembered that one, perfect weekend in collage. He'd found heaven with Rylee Kincaid and taking his pleasure with her had sent him straight to hell.

"Heard that before. I hope—"

The buzz of his intercom interrupted Glorie. He stabbed the button. "Yes?"

"Sorry to disturb you, Mr. Finnegan, but there's a Rylee Kincaid here. She's insisting on seeing you."

Hunter grinned. The bait had been taken, and the trap sprung. "Wait ten minutes, and then send her in."

"You're a bastard, Hunter."

A smile tugged at his lips. "Yeah, we're two peas in a pod."

She rolled her eyes, then narrowed them. "You really believe you can talk her into what you want?"

He rubbed his hands together in anticipation. "She'll do anything to save her company." And he'd do anything to make her listen to what he had to say. Memories of spanking her sweet ass ten years ago sent blood humming through him. For three nights and two sex-filled days, she'd been his.

His dick stirred. For ten years, he'd ached for her. Now, she was free, and he planned to claim her. By fair means or foul.

Glorie chuckled. "It will be entertaining and a pleasure to see the mighty Hunter Finnegan fall on his hands and knees for a woman."

"*I* won't be the one on my hands and knees." But he had fallen. Ten long, hellish years ago.

Also Read

Jonesin' for Action
SEALs On Fire

by

Samantha Cayto

Losing half a leg hasn't slowed down Aiden "Jonesin'" Jones. He can't deploy as a SEAL anymore, but that doesn't stop him from rising to the challenge of enjoying life as he always has. The one challenge left is to take a woman to bed. It's not his ability he questions, but his appeal. Can a woman overlook his damaged leg?

Marissa Nelson tends bar while working on her dissertation. Hooking up with customers isn't her style, but Aiden tempts her to break the rules. More than the sum of his parts, he's a man who can rock her world. But can she make him believe he's man enough?

Thank you for purchasing this
publication of The Wild Rose Press, Inc.
If you enjoyed the story, we would appreciate
your letting others know by leaving a review.
For other wonderful stories, please visit our
on-line bookstore at www.wilderroses.com.

For questions or more
information contact us at
info@thewildrosepress.com.

The Wild Rose Press, Inc.
www.thewilderroses.com

Stay current with The Wild Rose Press, Inc.
Like us on Facebook
https://www.facebook.com/TheWildRosePress
And Follow us on Twitter
https://twitter.com/WildRosePress